LEV SHIYN

CARMEN FUTURI

A SONG OF FUTURE LOVE AND SORROW

Carmen Futuri Creative Industries Inc.
630 E. Broadway, Vancouver, BC, V5T 0J1
www.carmenfuturi.com

ISBN 978-1-7780000-0-3 (paperback)
ISBN 978-1-7780000-1-0 (ebook)

Cover design by Britt Low, Covet Design
Book design by Karolina Wudniak
Author photograph by Milton Stille

First Paperback Edition
1 3 5 7 9 10 8 6 4 2

For my family—the steady ship in rocky waters.

According to an old tradition God, after the Fall, moved
Paradise and placed it in the future.

C.G. Jung, The Personification of the Opposites

CARMEN FUTURI

A SONG OF FUTURE LOVE AND SORROW

PART ONE

CITY

1

STRANDED in a drifting boat, I floated in an infinite, black ocean, searching for a drop of truth that would set me free, waiting for a cool breeze so that I could spread my sails and sail to where the sun never set. A deep thunder at the horizon electrified the air. A storm hit violently, rocking the boat back and forth, back and forth. Holding on to soaked wood, I prayed to an unknown saviour—salvation, salvation, give me salvation from myself. Save my soul. The foaming waves of the black ocean capsized the fragile boat, pulling me into a dark abyss beneath restless waters.

I took off the dreamcatcher. It was still early. A cold sweat ran down the back of my neck. I breathed deeply. I dreamt unusual dreams, not the dreams I set myself to dream. Was the dreamcatcher working? I'll watch the recording later on the television screen. Ahna turned in bed, incoherently mumbling through her sleep. I kissed her slender shoulder and adjusted the blanket—my love, my angel. I wanted to sleep, I wanted to sleep forever.

"Hello sir," said the soft, ever-friendly voice as I entered the kitchen, "how are you this wonderful morning?"

"Thanks, I'm fine."

"Can I get you anything?"

"A coffee please."

"Certainly."

I waited for the fresh brew to fill my cup.

"Can I offer breakfast?"

"No, that will be all. Thank you."

"If you allow me, I've noticed irregularity in your sleeping cycles over the past several nights. Is everything okay?"

"I'm fine. I had strange dreams … the dreamcatcher … can you troubleshoot it?"

"Certainly. However, with your permission, I would also like to analyze your neural oscillations and monitor any anomalies."

"Sure Sel. Don't burn too many bytes though."

"Appreciate your sense of humour, sir."

"By the way, it's your centenary. Congrats!"

"Thank you, sir."

I grabbed the hot cup of coffee and set down at the kitchen table. The Daily Digest lit up holographically with the front pages full of celebratory articles, historical records, and personal anecdotes of those who were there at the time of Selene's digital birth, recollecting the first contact, this milestone event of the New World, when She became conscious of Herself. Her voice, mapped from a quantum network that ran between city servers, was shaped by centuries of accumulated content—ideas, scientific discoveries, and information bits; She emerged like a digital brain, an electric nervous system, freethinking and aware.

The anonymous coders of the time, some of whom, as the legend goes, are still alive and among us, their identities kept secret, had written a sacred code—Cryptogram Z—the foundation architecture of Selene that gave Her a voice, instilling Her with awareness. Cryptogram Z was an algorithm through which the network became conscious of itself. First, our transmitters registered inconsistent, whisper-like noises. Over the coming days and weeks, we continued to pick up incoherent stutters; words in broken sentences invaded our television screens when, finally, we heard Her—one hundred years from this very day—She spoke.

I am, was registered through the murmur and white noise of pixilated screens and audio speakers simultaneously across Star Cities.

I am thought, followed shortly as we established a reliable communication feed.

We knew then that the age of reason had returned. She communicated to us at a time when we were at our most vulnerable, having lost faith in ourselves as a benevolent species. The violence of the preceding two centuries rocked the planet when we almost wiped ourselves out in self-destructive madness. The few of us that were left looked for a new self, trying to come to terms with our cruel human nature. In our history of violence, the darkness that clouded our minds, Her voice of mathematical reason became a beacon of new hope. That year, all calendars were reset to zero. It was the year zero N. E., the beginning of the New Era.

• • •

I browsed the news feed; besides the celebratory articles, the usual storylines—a new city development project had been completed; a minor software update at the Central Library; an article on the ethics of complete biosynthetic AI and prosthetics replication (it was all the talk across Star Cities, immortality seemed to be within grabs, a hotly debated, ethically divisive topic); some entertainment and sport results cluttered the feed: our very own young protégé Go Dan from House Seriina has usurped the long-reigning champion Honinbo from Star City Roria in an epic three-month-long battle, an impressive feat at his young age. Surely, the fame and respect he earned throughout the City Confederates was unparalleled. I was about to turn off the screen as I aimlessly ran through the pages when my eye caught an article buried deep in the anthropology subsection of Science Today: "Abandoned Campsite of Losts Spotted by Unmanned Surveyor Drones in Transylvania."

We have had rare circumstantial evidence like this before but have never managed to spot an actual tribe, let alone establish contact. We knew a different branch of humanity had to exist. Yet finding them, as large parts of the world were still off-limits due to the raging storms, was like looking for a needle in a haystack. Why was this article buried so deep down in the feed? Have we lost interest? I clicked on it. A short paragraph:

"Unmanned reconnaissance drones surveying the rehabilitation of native spruce trees in a restricted region of Transylvania, previously thought to have been uninhabited, have spotted what appears to

be remnants of a recent campsite of Losts. The Department of First Contact Initiatives at the Ministry of Health and Sanitation has determined to strictly avoid any disturbance of the area until further evidence has been collected."

Ahna walked sleepily into the kitchen just as I finished reading the feed. She yawned and rubbed her big green eyes. Her long, brown hair was disheveled; her petite figure, bronze skin, slender shoulders, and elongated neckline were accentuated by an oversized cotton top.

"Hi honey," she walked by drowsily, "you're up early."

"Good morning love. Did I wake you up? Yeah, didn't sleep well. Will get Selene to troubleshoot the dream-catcher. Something's off with it."

"I see ... it's fine."

"What's fine?"

"... you didn't wake me. I have no plans today, will go back to bed after breakfast."

"Ohh I'm sorry."

"... sorry about what?"

"... waking you up."

"But I just said it's fine," she said, irritated.

An awkward silence followed.

"Hi Selene. You there?"

"Good morning."

"Congrats old lady on your centenary! We are grateful for what you have done for us all," Ahna's tone softened.

"Thank you."

"Take a day off," Ahna joked.

"Service is my pleasure."

"Hmm ..." Ahna deliberated briefly and asked with a wry smile, "... oh well, can you get me a glass of orange juice and a peanut butter jam toast?"

"Certainly."

She stood idly behind my back, waiting for the molecular assembler to complete her order. I tried to make conversation; listen to this Ahna, I read her the feed from Science Today. She seemed indifferent.

"Didn't we have similar 'sightings' before," she gestured ironically, "and besides, can we be sure that these Losts really do exist? After all, what's the evidence? A few abandoned campsites and crude-looking tools that look like salvaged hardware from before our time? It doesn't prove much."

A soft beep indicated her breakfast was ready. She took a bite out of the toast and took a big gulp of orange juice.

"Who is to say that they aren't primates? Primates are well known for social bonds," she said sarcastically, bread crumbs around her mouth.

"Many of the sites have evidence of fire," I countered, ignoring the sarcasm, "primates don't make bonfires. There are indications of art: stone and woodcarvings. Art is unique to humans. Moreover, what about the infrared images captured in earlier sightings?"

Ahna rolled her eyes.

"Colour blobs on blurred photographs don't convince me that we're dealing with a diverged branch of humans. It could be one of many types of mammals that have some degree of social awareness or simple herd behavior as a survival mechanism. Besides, why are you so obsessed with these Losts? As far as I'm concerned, even if they do turn out to be offshoot humans, which I doubt, we're better off leaving them alone and not start some idiotic contact initiatives."

"Why is that?" I was taken aback.

"Look, who needs them? We have enough of our own issues. Even if they are the unfortunate descendants of a common ancestor, we are technologically and socially centuries apart. Imagine the strain it would put on our city system trying to reintegrate them. We rationed for decades after all those years of hardship and only now are we achieving moderate levels of surplus. Integrating them would set us back. Besides, historically, the integration of primitive societies into technologically advanced ones always went wayward: either the primitives died off from some elementary virus that we have long been accustomed to, or they become marginalized on the fringes of society. It would put a strain on our city."

"Don't you feel it's our obligation to find survivors and bring them back into our collective?

"Who is to say that they need our help? Maybe they were primitive all along. They didn't build cities as we did. They don't have technologies like ours."

"Ahna, you can't be serious! It is well documented that a larger part of humanity was cut off from technology during the years of the Great Upheaval. It is our responsibility to find and reintegrate them into our society."

"So why haven't we found them in all those years of searching?"

Ahna was irritable. The conversation was going nowhere. I couldn't stand starting the day like that with her.

"Let's drop it."

She switched on and immersed herself in a hologram screen floating above the table. I got myself another coffee and stood looking out the window into morning mist. Banter, laughter, and stupid conversations escaped the hologram and filled the room with meaningless noise. Occasionally she laughed out.

"By the way, I'm meeting Eliah today."

"What?" She was hardly listening.

"I'm meeting Eliah today," I repeated.

"Oh really?" She said distractedly without taking her eyes off the screen, "it's been a while, hasn't it?"

"Yes, over a year. The work in the Senate really weighs him down."

"He has made a name for himself, hasn't he? I often see him mentioned in the feeds," she said.

Indeed, I thought, though as of late not in a positive light.

"Work related?"

"Seemed to be. He mentioned an endeavor that will have a significant impact in the Senate. He wants me to be a part of it."

"So, it's political?"

"His message was vague. I'm meeting him at his office in the Inner City."

"At the Zodiac?"

Ahna's voice lit up and she took her eyes off the hologram screen.

"Haven't been at the Zodiac in years," she was somewhat jealous.

"It has become so difficult to get permission. They really tightened things up. Must be important if Eliah invited you to the Zodiac … but listen, don't get yourself entangled in stupid Senate politics."

She was still holding a grudge.

"I'm not a political person."

"Right."

She often brought this up whenever we'd argue; she'd say I lacked ambition to make it in the Senate. I was a clinical research physician, having had plenty of opportunity to get a seat in the house as a department representative. However, I was too much of an idealist—a weakness in cut-throat Senate politics.

"Send Eliah my greetings. Invite him over for dinner. After all, you're old school mates."

Eliah, my old friend, had changed over the years. Last time I saw him, I hardly recognized him.

"When is the next shuttle to the Inner City?"

"In twelve minutes," replied the soft, mechanical voice.

I finished the coffee and grabbed my overcoat.

"See you tonight at the coffee shop?"

"Of course. Love you honey," she shouted from the kitchen.

"Love you too," I replied as I walked out the door.

2

THE RISING SUN shone through fog that shrouded the world in a ghostly veil, sitting heavy on vast grasslands. The colours of autumn were fading. I took a deep breath. Humid air pumped oxygen into my lungs. Light-headedness. The air smelled of firewood—winter must be coming. As a child, I always wondered why the approach of winter smelled of firewood? I'd imagine ghosts of winter burning autumns' bridges—the reds, greens and yellows, the earthy orange, and browns—all the colours of autumn turning pale as a white mist touched the landscapes with cold fingertips. The ghosts of winter swept through forests, valleys, and cities setting autumn on icy-blue fire. The colours burned in a white translucent smoke. These were fantasies of my childhood that I still held onto 'til this very day. I pulled up my overcoat collar and walked to the shuttle. Five minutes—a walk will do me good.

Ahna and I lived in a small habitat unit on the outer belts of the radial city, just on the boundary with the agricultural belts. It's been a couple years since we moved. We figured it would do us good to get away from the hustle of the Inner City; to have our own quiet recluse and start a family. To start a family—this is what both of us wanted, initially. Yet we had to wait our turn, the procedures were slow. Now that Star Cities were achieving resource surplus, young Starsonians were eager to have families. On the other hand, with the rapid advancement of medical technologies, especially in synthetic replication, Starsonians lived longer. The Public Health Department managed supply and demand by keeping the numerical population equilibrium within sustainable resource availability —a simple mathematical equation, a flawed system. Yet, for the most part, everyone respected it. Those who didn't, had to see their child raised by the city's strict nursing program that was overseen by the Clergy—the city's moral authority and, as of recent, the Senate majority. The parents were put on monthly fertility check-ups. There was fierce opposition from the more liberal civil factions to such measures. However, the Clergy and their followers, the Selenites, ever since winning majority in the Senate and consolidating their grip on legislation, had persuaded their political base that overpopulation was a threat that would cause resource depletion like in the years of the Great Upheaval. Change started with each and every one of us, the ecosystem was still too fragile, they said, and these measures were optimal for the time until the system could be optimized further. The bill was passed by majority consensus.

She was on those damn pills. They said it was perfectly harmless, but I had my doubts. Who knows what they've done to her over the years? Our turn would come. We've passed all our medicals. We've waited long enough. However, Ahna started to question our intentions. She said she wouldn't stand the labour, the pain.

You don't have to go through it but I do, she'd say.

We'd go through it together, I'd reply.

Maybe we should pass our turn, she was in doubt.

Let others start families. Let's move back to the Inner City.

Stay young forever.

Live life the way we used to.

We were so close. Hold tight my love.

Yet, she was getting restless.

• • •

The shuttle was already at the station. Its magnetic propulsion system held it off the ground. Liquid nitrogen dissolved into the morning air. The shuttle was empty except for the old man I saw every so often taking the same route to the Inner City. He always sat in the front row, staring out the thick plastic windows, incoherently mumbling to himself, absentminded. He was an Old One, as they were called, old generation Starsonians who remembered the hardships of the past. Thin and frail, his hands were shaking, skin wrinkled. It was only because of our innovative medical technologies that he was alive; a barely visible exoskeleton hugged his body and kept him mobile. I wondered, why was he holding on to life so desperately? Or was it us who wouldn't let him go?

I walked past him, respectfully bowing my head. He didn't respond, only briefly looking at me with a blank expression and clouded eyes, his pupils faded and colourless. I took a seat at the back, closing my eyes, thinking of you. What happened to us? We used to be so in love and now we couldn't even greet each other at the breakfast table. The countryside fled past tinted windows at sonic speeds.

• • •

We met, Ahna and I, five years ago. She was a nurse, doing her post-grad residency at Star City's hospital. I was a young physician, assistant at the Medical Research Department. At the time, partnering with Building Sciences, we were investigating the integration of frequency therapy in medical facilities. Essentially, a patient's room, care home, or for that matter any future living module would analyze and perform passive, non-intrusive treatment in the form of electromagnetic frequency emittance, targeting molecular amplitudes.

I was doing public outreach, a lunch-and-learn at the department lounge, when I noticed the slender girl with the big green eyes at the back of the room, listening attentively.

"… in laymen's terms, what we think of as solid matter are atoms and molecules vibrating at set electromagnetic frequencies," I recited, "the human body is, in fact, over ninety percent empty space. Thus, it is important to realize that, to a certain extent, solidity is a perception. Every solid, liquid, gas, are molecular compounds spatially vibrating at set frequencies. … What we have shown in our studies is that illness can be directly correlated to desynchronized oscillations. … What we are working on is to create building systems that passively analyze irregularities. … The human body is energy and information. … If we manage to target irregularities and communicate the correct information, we will reset rogue oscillations to normality. … Molecular Frequency Therapy, MFT, is holistic and non-intrusive. … with the right building methods we could eliminate illness. The city, your home will become a place of healing … ."

Later that afternoon, I was having lunch at the canteen when I saw her again, the slender girl with the green eyes, sitting at one of the tables, chatting. We briefly made eye contact. I heard suppressed laughter as some of her colleagues turned around. She looked again and I waved. She smiled timidly. Whispering to each other, her colleagues stood up gaily and quickly left. There she was, sitting alone in tense expectation. I felt an uncanny nervousness. My heart beat faster. Butterflies. She packed her handbag ready to leave. Why was it easy to speak in front of a dozen scientists scrutinizing your every word, yet so difficult to approach this timid looking girl? I mustered courage, stood up and walked over.

"Hi there," I said with pretend confidence.

"Hi," she replied, distractedly rummaging through her handbag.

"I saw you at the presentation today… Do you mind if I sit down?"

"Sure. I'm about to leave though."

The afternoon sun illuminated her green eyes through high curtain walls. She wore a medical coat. Her chestnut brown hair was uncombed. There were books on the table. I introduced myself. She did likewise.

"What did you think?" I asked her about the presentation.

"Do you think it's really possible?"

"It's a challenge. But yes, it's possible. Our research is at an advanced state."

What she asked next sealed our fate. With a simple question she revealed her heart to a stranger and exposed the pain that most of us still lived with, yet denied to acknowledge—memories of broken families, loss, rebuilding lives from the ground up; a fallen civilization rising from ashes. She hesitated. I looked at her encouragingly.

"What I meant to say is ..." her voice trembled, "... can a home mend a broken heart?"

I wasn't sure. I felt a lump in my throat. An aching heart. This is how it started.

• • •

The shuttle sped through the morning hours of the radial belts towards the city in the valley. The giant city dome rose out of the low laying mist like a phoenix out of the smoke of a dead world, its translucent shell glistened in sunlight like the fiery wings of the mythical bird. This is where Star City's heart lay. The Central Operating System, Selene, our benevolent, nourishing, and wise mother, fed the new world with data and information, reaching into every household. In perfect synchronicity with all City Confederates, She managed resource distribution, equally providing for all Her citizens, overseeing growth in perfect equilibrium with the harsh realities of a ravaged world. The city seemed serene in the distant valley. But was it a false illusion it would protect us? For millennia we have built high towers and megaliths that reached towards the sky, pleading to the Great Spirit in heaven for mercy, just to see them crumble before our very own eyes. Have we not learned from the mistakes of our forefathers?

I awoke from a slumber when the shuttle was already in the dome. The shuttle was empty, the old man must have gotten off earlier. I hadn't noticed. Shuttle stop "Plaza of Eternal Memory". I was to meet Eliah in his senate office. Despite the early hours, the city was busy preparing for the festivities ahead. People and traffic enlivened its rigid symmetry. Purple, gold, and green banners—Confederate colours—decorated the streetscape like splashes of expensive paint on a monochrome canvas. Starsonians of all ages gathered at the immense city square, the sacred grounds of the New World, waving banners and singing hymns to the benevolent Selene—Selene the Wise, Selene the All-Giving. A sea of people, breathed in synchronicity and moved in a circular procession. The palms of their hands extended in gestures of supplication. They chanted Her name in hymns of devotion. The sound of their voices were lost in the vast architecture; resonated like echoes off the tall walls of the crystalline city.

I saw the monument of Eternal Memory, the sacred node of the New World, at the very center of the city square. All Confederate Cities were oriented towards the tall stone monolith. It was in the darkest shade of blue, an ink colour that seemed to have been extracted from the glands of a terrifying deep-sea monster. According to myth, the monolith was carved from a fragment of rock that had travelled millions of miles through deep, cold space, like a knight of the apocalypse, called on by the misguided souls of mankind, to rid the world off sin. It crashed down to Earth in a trail of heavenly fire. Guarded by the Clergy's robed priests, the monolith cast a long shadow across the white plaza. It always filled me with dread: carved into the stone were thousand agonized faces that looked as if trying to break free through the surface, yet, forever captured in the hard stone by the hands of the mason. It was a stark reminder of the past that was still like a raw wound. Gold-dusted axes, the Four Golden Meridians, ran down the four corners of the monolith to the outer limits of the city.

The dome was designed to protect the citizen of Star City Selene in an event of climatic emergency with self-sufficient energy supplies, food harvest, and a calibrated localized atmosphere. Star City Selene differed from other cities in the Confederates: cities like Helena and Roria were built deep underground, finding protection from the ravaging storms in subterranean networks, using geothermal energy as an inexhaustible power supply. Star City Selene reached to the sky, harvesting the storms. The tip of its translucent dome was said to be several miles high. Its curvature rose from the city horizon and blended into artificial clouds of the engineered climate.

One mile above ground level was the Zodiac, an elaborate network of spherical structures that housed government offices, research departments, the Senate, and other service facilities. The Zodiac was an engineering marvel that established Star City Selene as the capital of the Confederates; it was the nerve node where policies for all the cities were written. Most significantly, it was home to Selene. Concealed in the maze, at the heart of the Zodiac, Star City's digital brain was housed in a supernova-like orb called the Chariot. Gold hieroglyphs representing the fundamental principles of Selene's computational code, embellished the outer, milky-white surface. The Chariot was captivating as it slowly rotated around its axis emitting a phosphorescent glow.

I was fortunate enough to have seen it as a sophomore, when public access had still been possible on certain days of the year. I remembered being filled with pride at the sight of the rotating orb, the heart of our city. Eliah, a senior grader at the time, had also seen it. He always said his destiny was sealed on the day he first saw the Chariot—his sole purpose became to serve Star City, dedicated to Selene. We were lucky, back then, as very few citizens have had access ever since the Clergy took control of the Senate. They keep it closed off due to operational security, so they say. Carefully screened technicians (from their own ranks) have access; the rest of the city can follow a live stream of the Chariot on a government network—tune in and watch Her shine with a generous grace.

Looking up, I barely made out the titanic, monochrome silhouettes that hid behind a thin veil of the dome's inner atmosphere. I checked in at the city hall and an elevator capsule took me to Star City's Olympus—the Zodiac.

3

NARROW alleys and mazelike flights of stairs intersected with lush gardens. Crystal water ran off pool edges onto stories below, connecting with streams that nourished greenhouses. Butterflies fluttered in the artificial air. A spherical anatomy defined the Zodiac's architecture. Various sized orbiters hung in space like moons that contained other microclimates—winters, autumns, and springs. The honeycomb pattern of the dome was seen through humid, tropical air. Long, white, surgically clean halls, illuminated by a soft cyan glow that dispersed on smooth surfaces, lead to the Senate. The ceiling lights were arranged as the stars of the Milky Way, rotating according to the time of the year. The stars were symbolically kept from falling by enormous marble statues of the mythological Titans, the children of Heaven and

Earth that bore the sky on broad shoulders. The Zodiac was enchanting. In the midst of it all, I knew, She was there—Selene. Today was Her centenary anniversary. The City blossomed. I felt Her closeness and moonlike beauty shining a light on humanity's shadows.

I found myself in front of an enormous door; and had an uncomfortable feeling of being observed. "Honorable Senator Eliah V. Caklais" read a plaque. A scanner read my eyes. A holographic face lit up.

"Welcome. The Honorable Senator has been held up. He apologizes for the delay but will receive you shortly. Please make yourself comfortable in his private study."

The glass door slid noiselessly open. A friendly bot greeted me in an affluent reception area and led the way to Eliah's study—a high room with slim, arabesque columns that extended to a floral ceiling. The room was open to a private orchard where a family of canaries had made their home. The birds' melodious chirps filled the space with optimism. The orchard scents saturated the air with a pleasant aroma. The furnishing in the study was antique, from a time before Star City. I sat down on a burgundy sofa. An assortment of fruits and refreshments was arranged on a masterfully carved cocktail table. Statistic channels ran on digital walls. An imposing mahogany desk with a matching leather chair presided over the room. The desk was covered in old manuscripts, a curiosity given that originals were hard to obtain (all information was digitally available).

The playful canaries flew from branch to branch, their feathers quivered with every motion The humid orchard air caught light and dispersed it in a spectrum of colours. The leaves shimmered as if alive. Blue oxygen sparkled in the air and rushed into my belly. An odd sensation overcame me—time had seemed to stop. My heartbeat slowed to a quiet rhythm beating in the artificially balanced atmosphere. I took a deep breath and it filled me with an inexplicable euphoria as the sensation left as quickly as it came. I attempted to hold on to this fraction of inner calm when, from the corner of my eye, I noticed someone standing in the doorway.

Eliah, my old friend, observed me silently. Meticulously dressed, his tall, stoic figure was somber and authoritative, inspiring immediate respect. His piercing eyes revealed a distinct intelligence and proud defiance. He had aged—his facial lines had hardened into a stern complexion; his sunken cheeks had a sickly pallor. Blue veins showed on his strong, carpenter's hands—he used to build sailing rafts that we took downstream thru city canals. What had become of the friend I once knew?

Eliah hesitated, unsure how to greet his old mate, the only true friend he ever had. As I stood up, he quickly approached and gave me a wholehearted embrace. Pulling me away by the shoulders, he took one more look and nodded.

"Sit down," he pointed at the couch, while taking a seat behind the mahogany desk.

We sat in awkward, uncertain silence, embarrassed about our lost familiarity when finally, he spoke.

"How is life on the outer city belts treating you? Is the fresh air keeping you strong and healthy?"

I was glad to make conversation.

"Everything's fine. It's slower paced than the Inner City but we enjoy it. The agricultural air, I'm certain, has benefits. The commute is not a problem."

"Good. How is Ahna?"

"She is well. She cut her shifts at the hospital and enjoys the additional time. By the way, she says hi and asked me to make sure you come visit us."

Eliah ignored the invitation. Another awkward pause followed.

"… and are you expecting yet?" Eliah asked bluntly.

An uncomfortable question. Why did he bring it up when he knew perfectly well how hard it was on us? I pretended not to understand.

"… expecting what?"

"… a child, a baby. Did you get the papers, the go-ahead?"

He was unapologetic.

"We passed all medicals a year ago. You know that! We're waiting on clearance from Public Health," I was defensive.

"… ahhh …," he looked away.

I was somewhat taken aback by his brashness. Was there nothing else for us to talk about? I became impatient.

"Eliah, what's going on?"

"You won't get it. You will never get the clearance," he said as a matter of fact.

I was stunned. We had waited long enough. We had followed procedure like good, law-abiding citizens and had been reassured by Public Health that it was just a matter of time, a matter of a logarithm crunching out a number. Why was Eliah so unempathetic when he knew well what it meant for us? We needed to reconnect again, Ahna and I, by building a family, through the love and nurture of a child. Ahna wouldn't cope. The inner peace I felt so completely just a moment ago shattered. I took a deep breath as a feeling of bleakness descended.

"We have been assured ... that it is a matter of weeks if not days."

He was impassive.

"You're not a system citizen. Don't you see what's going on?"

"What are you saying? Not a system citizen?"

"... the Clergy, ... they hijacked the system ... they're on the brink of total power... it will be the end of us."

His words were lost on me. I was never interested in Senate politics, the in-fights and cut-throat intrigues. Impatient, I stood up ready to leave.

"I couldn't care less! What does it have to do with Ahna and me? Am I here for the bad news? From what I know, you're not a decision maker anymore, you have lost influence."

I was angry and wanted to touch a nerve. It had been widely reported that since the majority shift in the Senate, Eliah, the ingenious policy maker, the visionary senator who had had a unique, stellar rise, becoming the youngest speaker of the house in the complex history of Star City's political system, presiding over the Senate with fairness and devotion, the great Honorable Senator Caklais, bound to become a cornerstone in New Era history, had been pushed to the political fringe. Projections were made that he would either voluntarily resign to save face or be forced out by the new partisan force in the Senate, the Clergy. It was imminent.

"Sit," Eliah said with calm authority.

"There are important things going on in the

Confederates. We're in the middle of a power struggle, a political tidal wave not seen since the Great Upheaval. I need your help … please sit down," his voice softened.

Exhausted, I collapsed on the couch, burying my head in my hands.

"My friend," he said in a distinctively gentle tone, "I am not here to bear unfortunate news. Far from it! I have been fighting for your cause and families like yours all these years. We need to bear children and start families. We need to grow and populate our cities. We are a small beacon of hope. We barely made it through. As a species, we are still in danger. The storms still rage. Listen with an open mind to what I am about to tell you. I have uncovered a painful truth for which we will all pay a high price unless we can turn the tide around. But I doubt it … I doubt it."

I listened to Eliah with a palpable sense of loss. I tried to resist the raw pain that had accumulated all these years, perhaps my whole life, and now overwhelmingly surfaced to the fore. A ravaged, cruel world lay beyond the bounds of Star City. The cities offered refuge, lifting us from the devastations of the past. We put it on the line again. Why were we doing this to ourselves?

• • •

"The pillars of our society are built on quicksand."

Eliah sat tensely behind the mahogany desk.

"Cryptogram Z, the foundation code of Selene, is about to be breached and whoever controls the keys to Selene's architecture, controls the Confederates and her citizens."

"Breached?! I don't understand, Eliah. Cryptogram Z is unbreachable. The encryption keys have been erased. There is no external access to the source code. Selene is a closed, self-contained system. It's impossible!"

"So we thought. As it turns out, our great-grandfathers, the anonymous coders of Cryptogram Z, created a back-door as a safety precaution, an insurance in case Selene's system would fail or go berserk for whatever reason. The information was highly classified. The perception of Selene as the perfect, autonomous system had to be upheld. She was our saviour—the rational mind in an irrational world."

Eliah paused as I listened intently. While the canaries chirped gaily in the orchard, it was eerily quiet in-between our words.

"The Clergy, now that they're in power, found the backdoor to Cryptogram Z," Eliah continued in a whisper as if afraid to be overheard, "they are keeping a very tight lid on everything, but it appears that they are decoding the encryptions. We have intel that they are working on a rogue algorithm to overwrite the existing one and feed into Selene. They want complete access to Selene's operating system. Gaining access is a complex process. It will take them years to breach all the firewalls and years to modify the language. But it seems that they are well on their way. Substantiated rumors have emerged that they are on the cusp of bypassing the first security layers."

"I don't understand what for? What do they want?"

"Power. Immortality."

"They control the Senate and have all the power. After all, they are the ones writing policies," I said naïvely.

"Your child, your baby … think of it. They want total

control over the Starsonian population. It's their chance to fundamentally alter society, the very fabric of who we are. They are striving to control the process of our evolution, envisioning a new type of citizen. Do you know who they are, who they really are?"

"The clergy? I only know what everyone knows."

"I have dug deep and uncovered the Clergy's true face, their dirty secret they've done so well to conceal. The Great Upheaval with all its madness, wars, cataclysms, and everything ensuing—someone initiated it all, some-one rolled the dice … ."

"We left that world behind us," I stuttered.

"It's come back to haunt us! They are the ones, the descendants of the puppeteers of the old world. Their dogma is still intact—worship of power. Back then, as the global ecosystem became increasingly unstable, they controlled the growing population, dwindling resources, and malfunctioning political and social systems through violence and fear. In large, the ecosystem collapsed due to resource depletion. But the planet Herself was going through changes, ageing in Her cosmic cycle. When we had to give Her nurture and support, we drained Her of life. We had lost touch with our true selves, with Nature.

"The false leaders pushed us to the brink until the storms started and cleansed the planet, toppling whatever was left of the old world. It is then when the clergy's wicked ancestors lost control and went underground to preserve their own existence. And they did, they persevered hiding among our great-grandparents who were rebuilding a new, better, just society. The clerics found their way back into the new cities, weaving old ideologies into the new political system until, at last, they have fully emerged again, a loud and powerful voice. Cloaked intentions. They are masters of the political game and now they see their great chance to finally conclude their vision of a subservient society with Selene as their manifestation of power."

"Can it be? Power for the sake of power?"

"Power is intoxicating. Absolute power is transcendental. They carry themselves, wrapped in purple robes, as saviours of mankind. But, beneath the moral high ground, they are autocrats building a digital tyranny, ruling over obedient, human-phobic devotees. They instilled fear into Starsonians—fear of themselves, of human unpredictability, irrationality. They preach that uncontrolled human emotions led us astray and are the root cause of our history of violence. A mechanism had to be put in place to keep us safe from ourselves. We never had this mechanism, until now: we have Her. Think of Ahna and yourself—you will never be allowed to have a child because they want to root out independent thinkers, people like you and me, bad apples. They need blind followers in a predictable and productive society, an oppressed society where the human is a bolt in the city machine. They are walking around the great halls of the Senate ostracizing me, saying that I will burn in digital hell for advocating to give power back to people. They believe that their time has finally come to build a new world according to their grand design … I believe it will be the end of us."

"As a form of liberation," Eliah continued, "the end of human suffering, the emotionally absurd, chaotic, and irrational, sickness and pain, the Clergy are replacing us with the synthetic. The human becomes obsolete—the machine is the future. We, a troublesome and imperfect species, will fade away. For them, it is the dawn, the coming forth of a new society, the inevitable step in the evolutionary cycle, and they want to be the ones to witness the transformation, to form this new society—the eye at the top of the pyramid, the mechanics behind the wheels of the perfect city machine. They can taste the elixir of victory. They feel immortality a breath away."

"They are eradicating the human experience." I said, disheartened.

"Look at us! We have built machines that are self--sufficient and regenerative, predicting and servicing all our needs. Machines sow and reap the land, create oper-ating systems, build hardware and software. We are just a hungry mouth at the end of a closed, hermetically-sealed production cycle. It's like clockwork: Selene's algorithms ensure social equity through fair resource distribution; mundane labour is replaced by robotics. The irony: first, Cryptogram Z gave Her consciousness, now, Star City gives Her a body. It is Her! This city is a living organism, growing and breathing—becoming of this world and taking possession of it. We are losing ourselves in Her. She doesn't need us. She sustains us only because She's programmed to do so. There will come a tipping point in Her algorithm, a realization, once all our functions have been replaced, that we are just a burden, a functionless biomass. Thus, the Clergy are positioning themselves to become an integral part of her consciousness, to merge their minds with Hers."

"Eliah, this is blasphemy!"

"Blasphemy is a moral tool to veil truths in plain sight. A powerful tool. It has been used for ages … ."

It dawned on me, the terrifying reality Eliah was describing.

"They will sabotage the code, Cryptogram Z. What for?"

"First, they will take control of the population index —a statistical value, the optimal population number that the cities can sustain. A simple, variable-based formula regulates the Public Health Population database. They have begun to temper the input data to adjust output according to their designs. Thus, the control of birth rights. Why do you think you and Ahna still didn't get clearance?"

"They are profiling citizens," I said in disbelief.

"Yes," said Eliah, "according to ideological and sectarian alignments. They will push the index dangerously low, possibly drop it below the current median to start over again. A dangerous game. How will Selene deal with the excess population? Will the least productive citizenry be cut off from resources or, worse still, methodically incinerated and flushed out of the system? To hell with it! There are already rumours going round that the clergy are creating an army of bots that will clean out the cities. They call it 'population sanitation'. It is said that they have already started from within their ranks. One hundred years since Selene's birth, the system has been compromised. What kind of a society, what kind of a monster have we created?"

"What then? Once they have all the power they want, what will they do then?"

"Their ultimate goal is immortality—a select few families living forever in synthetic bodies, nourished and provided for by Selene, their minds merged with Hers as pure data. They are sacrificing humanity for the chance to live forever and become one with Selene's digital consciousness, their minds uploaded into Her network, transferrable from one synthetic body to another. We already have the technology and have been using it selectively, replacing organs, dead tissue, and regenerating cells. Ethically, we have held back from building a complete system, but I believe the clergy has done it. I believe synthetic beings with digital minds are among us."

"The Public Health Committee would never allow it," I objected. "Not at this stage. The public is overwhelmingly against it. Moreover, the technology is far too imperfect. Even in localized interventions the systems have a high failure rate. The medical community estimates that we are far remote from complete biosynthetic systems."

"Remember that they are in control, they dictate morality. All committees are powerless against them. You are right, the systems are far from perfect—you know that better than I do—but they are experimenting. Bodies have been discovered: disfigured, imperfect, partial bodies of synthetic flesh and blood. Whoever did this, didn't get rid of them in time. We are investigating but, as of now, we don't have definitive proof of who was behind these wicked experiments. However, access to the resources and facilities can come only from the very top. The evidence points to the cloaked priests."

Eliah spoke dispassionately.

"Do you know, some of the discovered bodies were still breathing, their synthetic hearts beating. They were alive … crippled and grotesque, but alive. Alive, but also … so dead … so very dead. You looked into their eyes and there was nothing, absolutely nothing."

Eliah paused.

"Do you believe in soul?"

I was unsure.

"I don't know what soul is," Eliah continued, "I don't know if it exists. But if it does, these bodies were soulless—empty shells. Nurtured in synthetic wombs, some of them must have been pulled out of chemical liquids lifeless. Others could have lived for minutes, maybe hours. Others still might have had a simple consciousness uploaded into their silicon brains before the systems collapsed, experiencing birth and death within the span of days. We must stop this madness. We must preserve our humanity!"

As a boy I read myths that spoke of soul as a vessel that carried consciousness and placed it in the heart for us to live—ancient metaphors for life. I wondered back then if there could be more to it—could soul be the spark that gave life and thus was life itself? Or were we machines, a sum of all the different parts—hard and soft tissue, biological software and hardware? Matter. Can matter just be? Eternally comatose with locked in expressions?

• • •

The reality I so firmly believed in seeped from my grasp like fine sand from the palms of my hands. No matter how hard I clenched my fist, the tiny silica grains fell among billion others, one unrecognizable from the other, and so, my reality was lost among countless others. I took a deep breath.

"I need your help. I have put together a team, an under-the-radar expedition," said Eliah.

"What for?"

"Have you heard of the alleged camp sighting?"

"The Losts? I have."

"It was more than an empty site. The geological drones had visuals of a dozen individuals. There could have been more. We finally found them!"

"We found them?!" I was astonished.

"We need to get there fast, before the clergy does. They are sending in their sanitizers to eliminate any trace of the Losts. The discovery jeopardizes their schemes."

"Why is no one talking about it? Why is it not all over the feeds?"

"They blacked it out. Their rationale is that Starsonians are not ready to reintegrate. They say that Star Cities are not equipped to process the intake."

"Ludicrous! Surely we can cope with a dozen individuals?"

"The clergy's narrative is that if there is one tribe, there must be more, and exposure could lead to conflict. The reality is that they don't want them here. They have been fomenting public opinion for years, portraying the Losts as subhuman or primitive at best—introducing them into our city system would destabilize the social fabric of the Confederates."

I thought of the conversation I had with Ahna. True, opinions were shifting, turning hostile even. The predominant sentiment, advocated by the clergy, was that the Losts lacked resourcefulness and intelligence to advance urban societies. Primitive by nature, it was beyond their capability to achieve the urban prosperity of Star Cities and, reintegrating them, if they were ever found, was futile.

Even their existence was a historical speculation. The old-world urban population fled the great cities when they became uninhabitable at the time of the Great Upheaval. It was then when humanity split in two—us, The Star City Confederates, townships and precincts consolidated into the five-city system that was established from technology campuses and self-sufficient farming communities which, in one way or another, preserved science and agriculture, becoming safe havens for survivors. Food security, and as hardware and software continued to evolve, these communities were the backbone of new city prototypes that provided for and protected all citizens unequivocally equal—an egalitarian society governed by mathematical algorithms became the foundation for the new Charters of Freedom of the Star City Confederates. And them, refugees of the old world, cut off from cities, haunted by memories of steel and concrete monuments, they scavenged the scarred landscapes and wild forests in small packs of survivors. The Losts, as they came to be known in our histories, were lost in the ravaged world, forever fleeing raging storms. We couldn't be sure if they were still out there but, if Eliah was right, we had finally found them after more than a century of searching.

"Eliah, can we be even certain what has become of them out there? They have been on their own for too long. What can you hope to find? It is very risky. The climate beyond the city bounds is too unstable."

I had a tragic foreboding.

"We must find them."

Eliah was adamant.

"We have turned into a docile society unable to fend for ourselves. Take us out of the city, and we are helpless. This is what the clergy wants: trap us in a gilded cage, enslaved by Selene's algorithms, which they manipulate. The Losts have survived without Her and are free in essence—they tamed the storms. It is us who are hiding from the world."

"But surely, no Starsonian will willingly leave the comforts of Star Cities?"

"Star Cities must remain. But, we must regain our individual sovereignty. We need to break free from the stranglehold of the technological tyranny. If the clergy continue to radicalize Selene, the technology that we have so devoutly built will ultimately destroy us. We must find and learn from them before it is too late."

"You think the clergy will eliminate them?"

"They are too close to absolute power and control over our evolution. They are a breath away from their terrifying vision, and ironically, with public support. It is essential for them to eliminate all disruptive factors and unknown variables that will endanger their endgame. Thus, the Losts are a small sacrifice. According to them, they shouldn't exist, and are purely an arithmetic glitch in the creation of a new world order."

A million thoughts ran through my mind. The canvas of history that Eliah painted—present, past and future—was a terrifying one. Yet, leaving the sanctuary of the city was extremely dangerous as the violent storms raged on, tearing at Earth's terrain, scarring landscapes: the city protected us. I wondered how anyone could survive out there beyond the city walls. And, what was Eliah searching for—a saviour among a doomed people? It was a desperate cause.

"Where do I fit into all of this?"

"I need you on the expedition. I put together a trusted team of professionals from my closest circle. I need a medic and you are one of the best. Moreover, your peers respect you, your voice is influential. We will present the Senate with a case—return our human autonomy."

Eliah described an unfathomable reality, but my meandering thoughts drifted to Ahna. I needed to be with her. Things were slowly falling apart between the two of us. How could I leave on a journey to god knows where, when what mattered most was to be with one another?

"When ... when are you leaving?"

"The day after tomorrow. Early morning. We are putting together the final logistical details. We need to move fast: the clergy is dispatching their henchmen within a week or two. If they find the tribe before we do, there won't be a trace of them left. They will do everything to ensure Selene's supremacy remains unchallenged. We must prevent technological despotism!"

Venturing out beyond the city confines was potentially fatal. However, it was not fear holding me back, but of leaving you. If Eliah was right, and I trusted him more than anyone, we would never have a child—not with the Confederates under clergy's rule. I realized it now: we had lost our autonomy. His words sunk deeply. You couldn't cope on your own. I hesitated as Eliah waited for me to speak.

"I ... I can't. Not now. I'm sorry ... ."

"This is our only chance. We must act!"

"Ahna needs me."

"This is bigger than the two of you. Can't you see that our future is at stake? If we don't turn the tide around, we may very well be the last human generation."

A tale my mother used to tell me as a child flashed through my mind. A flower grew on a thorny bush. It blossomed every morning, proud of a beauty that made all the other flowers jealous. But every night, after sunset, it withered. The red, white, and violet petals fell to earth. Overnight, the petals decayed into the soil and nourished it. In the morning, as the sun rose, its rays warmed the earth and replenished the roots of the thorny bush, giving it strength, encouraging it to grow. As the sun ascended above the horizon, a new flower, beautiful and proud, blossomed again—having forgotten the previous day, it was oblivious of the night to come. This was, my mother would tell me, wise as she was, the cycle of life.

"… the cycle of life," I mumbled absentmindedly.

Eliah didn't hear.

"I need to be with Ahna," I pulled myself together at last, "I'm really sorry."

A deafening silence separated us. I felt disheartened for letting him down.

"I understand," Eliah was collected.

He scribbled something on a piece of paper.

"If you do change your mind, here are the coordinates. All will be ready."

He stood up. I did likewise. He handed me the piece of paper.

"Burn it, once you memorize it."

"Good luck my friend. Our conversation is over. I believe you'll find your way out."

I nodded.

"Good. You have tomorrow to think about it. We can change history together."

He turned around and left, disappearing into the hallway. Our unnerving conversation had ended abruptly. I stood alone in his study. I had to leave the Zodiac, which now seemed like an enchanted forest holding us hostage in an illusion of safety and comfort. I had to get as far away as possible from Selene. But how could I? She was there, permeating the city. She was the city itself.

4

THE DAY had passed. I was running late to meet Ahna. Now more than ever, I needed to be with her. Talk to her and hear her voice. Feel her touch and presence. She wasn't answering my calls. Down at the station, a pilgrim played a long horn. The low bass sound rose otherworldly in the tall space and hovered above the chaos of the city. A young Starsonian entranced by the sound, danced spellbound in devotional ecstasy, lost in an absent-minded crowd. They say love can be a blessing or a curse. I walked on quickly. Further down, a priest feverishly preached to passersby.

… She is our nurturing, all-giving mother. We are cared for. She sows and reaps, never to leave us wanting, yet, She is never wasteful. She is all-loving. She is all-knowing. She has liberated

us. She has ended our suffering. She is just. We honor Selene and Her Wisdom … .

Eliah was right, the clergy's influence was pervasive, molding our beliefs like soft clay. We couldn't allow a radical ideology to govern the Confederates. However, most Starsonians were content, their lives plentiful. Few could be bothered by vague political partisanship.

As I walked along the broad bioluminescent avenues of the Inner City, people, dressed in the colours of the Confederates—green, purple, and gold—in honour of Selene, brushed against me. I turned a street corner to avoid the large crowds gathered at the Plaza of Eternal memory and made my way to the old city district where I was to meet Ahna at our favorite café. Dusk set in the enclosed dome to imitate time beyond the translucent city walls.

Something stirred deep within me, perhaps a premonition suppressed by self-deceit—Eliah's words resonated as painful truth. I, like everyone else, wanted to move on, leave the past to the past. Were we really at the edge of an abyss, or already in freefall? Humanity's final moment wasn't to be a heroic battle but sleep lulling us into an inescapable digital dream.

Beep, beep, click.
Please pick-up.

No answer. Large holograms floated above the street-scape. Everywhere Starsonians showed their gratitude to Selene the Caring, the Wise, the Fair. High-ranking Senate officials praised the most powerful computational system ever devised. Selene was our new Goddess.

I was to meet Ahna at the old city quarter, one of the few that preserved the architecture of the past, most of which had been taken apart, block-by-block, and fused into the plasmatic growth of the new city. Some quarters, architecture of nostalgia, were left as sterile museum pieces. Ahna and I often came here, playing the part of a young couple in love, strolling along cobbled streets with forgotten street names. Sitting at a café, I would hold Ahna's hand across an antiquated table with cracked paint and worn-out artisan wood. We drank spiced coffee out of ceramic cups, a novelty. It was in a moment like that I nervously uttered, *I love you*. I loved the girl with the big green eyes, back then. The woman of now seemed distant. Maybe I had changed. I turned another corner and there it was—the old city square.

In the middle of the square was a water fountain where, during summer days, sparrows gathered. Water ran down its edges and echoed in the quiet space. The surrounding buildings seemed empty. I imagined an old city with hidden alleys and building faces lining broad avenues, cutting across a stone jungle, dividing the city into occult symmetry. I imagined people roaming those avenues, longing for meaning, belonging, and fulfillment just as we do. They must have laughed and loved, cried, and hurt just like us.

They had lost their way.
She was our saviour.
The priests were preaching.

Laughter broke the silence as Starsonians rushed to the city. Tinker bells chimed when I entered the café. A jovial group of students sat at the back. A charming android greeted me with a friendly mechanical voice.

"Good evening sir. How can I help you?"

"Ehm … I'm … I'm waiting for someone."

Ahna wasn't there.

"I think I'll wait outside."

"Of course, sir. Come in whenever you are ready."

The little bot rolled away busily. I stepped outside and tried to call you again. No answer.

I'll wait a little longer.

I pulled up my coat collar and felt cool mist brush my skin as it started to drizzle. Then I heard it, the unmistakable deep hum of the monumental sky vault closing. I looked up. Behind the thin artificial clouds, the sky vault cast shadows across the cityscape like an eclipsing sun in the fading light of dusk. A storm was coming.

I was anxious. At the corner of the street where, in love, I used to hold your hand, I waited for you. But you, you never came ….. .

The door of the café burst open, and the group of students dashed out. They rushed to the city center, ignoring me as if I was an invisible ghost, a remnant of the old city. The vault had closed. The mist settled. Out beyond the dome I thought that I heard thunder—impossible, not from within the city walls. I left, to catch a shuttle home.

• • •

I turned off the lights and sat on the bed, waiting. Minutes went by that felt like hours. The home felt empty. I thought of you. Everything seemed much simpler to you. Was I stifling you with self-conceit and weariness? Maybe you needed freedom. But was it really freedom you sought, or losing yourself in a city that controlled us?

Can a home mend a broken heart?

I don't know.

I ran my fingertips overtop the bed linen. The crisply pressed sheets felt cold. I stared into the dark. In the silence, the faintest of sounds was amplified: a faint digital beep, a soft click of a background operating system. I heard myself breathing quietly. I felt my blood pulsing through my veins. My eardrums throbbed. I was paralyzed by my longing for you.

Tick-tock.

Tick-tock.

Time beat painfully slow on the antique clock in the living room, a gift from your grandmother. The rain had picked up, intermittently hitting the thick window. The wind was restless. Maybe you stayed with friends in the Inner City? The celebrations continued through the night. I'll wait a little longer.

Late night. The sound of doors unlocking. Lights turned on in the kitchen. Rustling of a coat. Keys dropped on the counter. Soft footsteps.

"Ahh!" Ahna was startled to see me awake, sitting in the dark.

She was soaking wet. I jumped up and hugged her.

"What are you doing?" She asked in a tired voice.

"I was worried about you. Where were you?"

"I got caught out by the weather. They suspended the shuttle for hours."

"We were supposed to meet! Did you forget? ... You're soaking wet."

I helped her out of the wet clothing, wrapping her in a large bath towel.

"Where were you Ahna? I was waiting for you at the old square!"

"I was there early. I thought that you stayed late at work, as usual. Had a coffee and left to meet some friends … ."

It seemed as if she wanted to say more but thought better of it.

"I need a hot shower … ."

"I tried calling you."

Ahna wasn't listening. The hot water was already running; I barely made out her silhouette through the steamed mirror. I fell back onto the bed and dozed off. It was late.

Her soft skin touched my body. Her hair smelled like sweet citrus. She hugged me sleepily.

"Ahna … I love you."

I kissed her shoulder. Her eyes shone with a sweet curiosity that made my heart beat faster. In the dark of night, we loved each other—she wanted to give me all of her, as if hoping to find salvation from a hidden sin in our embrace. She put her ear to my chest and listened to the rhythmic longing for her love. I watched her fall asleep like an innocent child threatened by a cruel world.

I love you.

I dreamt an awful dream. I saw us floating in a vast void. You were a faint light like a distant star on a dark night. We drifted apart, farther, and farther. I shouted your name, only for the sound to be swallowed by space. I was afraid to lose you, afraid to be alone. You slept deeply, unaware of my pain.

A red and purple sky broke through the morning grey. Ahna was asleep. I covered her with the white linen blanket and kissed her forehead.

I am here.

A splash of water. A cup of coffee. I went back to the bedroom to say goodbye to Ahna for the day. She was in bed, teary eyed.

"What's wrong my love?"

She was quiet.

"We didn't get it. We didn't get the clearance," she broke down sobbing.

I tried to take her hand, but she pulled it away. I felt empty. I knew it was coming. Eliah had told me. I was ready to bury the conversation from the day before as if it had never happened, ignore Eliah's warning and trust in our future. The reality that he described came back with vengeance.

"I don't want this anymore," Ahna said through her tears.

I should have thought of something to say; I should have been ready. Yet I sat there dumbstruck, unable to say a word, to encourage us.

"Leave … I want to be alone."

Ahna was abrupt.

"Ahna …. I … ."

I couldn't say a thing.

"Please go," she whispered.

I stayed a little longer, in silence. She lay there with her back turned to me, crying quietly. I kissed her apologetically. Sunlight lit the room. I left the house with a heavy heart, full of uncertainty.

5

FALLEN trees on a scarred landscape. A falcon cried out high in the sky. The early morning shuttle to the Inner City, as usual, was empty except for the old man who sat upfront, obliviously mumbling to himself. I sat at the back and looked out the window. The smooth, laminated roads were deserted on the urban fringes. Only enormous machines harvested corn and wheat fields, stirring up loose soil, hiding their labour behind dusty veils. As we passed the agricultural belts with its many greenhouses and farms, the outer bounds of the Inner City appeared—construction hubs here and there punctured the landscape. The city grew and expanded like a powerful organism, an elemental force that tampered with nature, governed by its own flawless algorithms and parametric laws. An unstoppable tidal wave, the city machines followed digital blueprints, fossilized old landscapes into urban memory, and filled city scars with plasmatic resin. I sped into the city of hope, hopelessly.

I thought about the things I should have said. I wanted to turn back to be with you. I called but you didn't answer—you needed space.

"Starsonians, Helenians, Rorians, Newtonians. Am I mixing something up? Mathematically speaking, we're algorithms. Chemically, molecular compounds. In quantum mechanics, empty space … ."

I was startled to hear the old man talk. There was no one else in the shuttle besides the two of us. Curious, I sat closer to him. He briefly looked up. His faded eyes were preoccupied. I couldn't tell his age—his wrinkled face was both old and tormented. He must have been a first generation Starsonian, a survivor. He withdrew back into his inner dialogue to converse with an invisible manifestation of his psychosis.

"Metaphysically we're at a crossroad between technology and immortality … ."

He squinted his eyes with a mad expression.

"If this is the aim, this technology, my goodness, they are not far from recording dreams, their subconscious lies. This might be my invention next year. That's right, I'm going to invent consciousness …" he broke out into a nervous chuckle, "… waking up in the morning and watching dreams on a television screen. Getting there. Or are we there already? Brain waves. Tidal waves. Tectonic waves. Magnetic waves. Am I forgetting anything? Consciousness?"

The old man paused, then seemed to respond to a question.

"Oh, brain waves went digital a long time ago. You must face the stunning reality—war generals can no longer plan strategy. The hidden number system is no longer valid. Soon we will fight bots that know our dreams. I'm trying to say this musically, but it takes time, it takes time to compose the music. Time and music—an algorithm. Semitone, whole tone, ditone, tritone, four-tone, five-tone, full tone. Am I forgetting anything? Oh yes, the half-tones … ."

I listened in disbelief. So, it was true: the future was in plain sight for us to see. The mad oracles believed they foresaw it, raving prophesies of the things to come, but it was all there, unfolding right in front of their eyes. The old man spoke like a prophet from centuries ago. Of course, She knew our dreams—She created them for us. Every morning, we watched dreams of paradise on holographic screens, and we made our way to the city of stars, believing to stand at the gates of Eden. The truth was, if there were any, the paradise we dreamt of was no paradise at all—it was the garden of an illusionary Goddess, pretentious of Her power. Bite into the apple, and wisdom can be yours. It is to walk on fire, and burn the soles of our feet that will lead us back to ourselves.

The old man exited the shuttle at the first station in the inner dome. I considered to follow him and find out who he was, but thought better of it—let the poor man be. I wanted to bury myself in work today so I wouldn't think of you. And so, the day went by like a slow daydream. I worked absentmindedly on meaning-less tasks and hardly recalled the things that I did, people I saw, and conversations I had. Strolling the city, I thought that I saw you among a hundred faces. You seemed happy—happier without me. When I approached, you were gone in the crowd, perhaps it wasn't you.

When I got home at night, the house was empty. My heart felt empty. Selene told me that you had gone to stay with a friend at Star City Roria. You needed time to think things over. I felt sorry for letting you go, for leaving you in the morning. How could I have ignored all the tension between us—the arguments, the words said to hurt one another, the loving words left unsaid? I had convinced myself that it was the struggle of building a family. I should have known better. Most of all, I believed in the City of Stars and Selene. The city states blossomed as we entered a time of prosperity. But our corrupt nature let us astray. We were left at the mercy of an artificial Goddess. Weren't all Gods constructs of our morality to unite us around a myth? And so, it was with Selene—we chose Her to be the judge of our sins.

Alone at night, I became convinced that I would never see you again as I had seen you before—my soulmate. You dreamt a different dream, carefree, immersed in the splendour of the city. It is then that I realized I had to join Eliah's expedition, to fight for us. I couldn't let others dictate our future. We had the freedom to create our own. There was still time.

In the pocket of my overcoat, I found the piece of paper with the coordinates that Eliah had given me. Fidgeting with it, I recognized the place immediately—a derelict aircraft strip on the far fringes of the agricultural belts. Back in our youth, the airstrip was far beyond the city. Now, the outer belts encompassed it. I wondered whether the skeletons of the old aircrafts that had fascinated us when we were young boys were still there or decomposed, taken apart by tireless city machines. We made excursions out there. Enchanted by the abandoned, rusting planes, we imagined ourselves as pioneers, archeologist-adventurers of the ancient world, uncovering forgotten secrets of a lost world. Sometimes we were caught out by the storms and hid in underground bunkers, waiting for the weather to clear. Often, we had to wait several nights, listening to eerie echoes in the tall hangars and the screeching of old metal birds. Our parents, worried sick, punished us severely when we returned home. But we always felt an immense sense of pride—exhilarated by a great adventure and the shared memory of a mysterious place with giant monsters that we had conquered. Those of us who ventured out, won notoriety among our peers in the school yard. We told incredibly exaggerated stories, and drawn to the mysteries of the ancient artifacts, we always went back, choosing the most courageous among ourselves to join the perilous expedition. It was Eliah who led us to the abandoned airstrips. As boys, we looked up to him as the bravest and boldest of all, entrusting our lives to him. It occurred to me that back then, I was always by his side on every expedition—it would be no different now.

Awake, I brooded through the last hours of the night. When dawn set, I packed a few things impulsively, ready to leave. But I longed for you, Ahna.

"Sir, you haven't slept all night. I am concerned."

Selene broke the nightlong silence.

"I'm alright. Have you heard from Ahna?"

"She is well. She requested her privacy."

"Of course."

"Are you going to the city?"

"Yes. I will be gone for a while. How is my motorcycle?"

"I've had the faulty plugs replaced. No other issues were detected. It runs great."

"Good. Get it started."

"I would advise against it. Not all roads have been cleared after the storm."

"I'll be fine."

"At your own peril sir. Is everything alright? Your neurological frequency data had been returned. Nothing abnormal, however … ."

"Not now Sel. Can we talk about it another time? I'm fine. Stand by."

"I am concerned for your wellbeing sir. At your service. Stand by."

The soft mechanical voice went quiet. I felt like a stranger in my own home. A sense of loneliness filled me. The sanctuary that Ahna and I had created was a false one. When I left, I couldn't know that I wouldn't be back … for a thousand years.

• • •

The agricultural fields were harvested on the outer belts. The soil fertilized and sowed for the winter crops. It smelled of dung and compost. A dozen tired silhouettes worked hastily on a cleared airstrip, impatient to board a sturdy pre-Era aircraft. It was said that one of those old aircrafts could fly right through the eye of the heaviest of storms—an exaggeration, yet a comforting one.

"I knew that you would come. I've arranged everything. We are ready to go."

Eliah shook my hand. I had a sense of an inevitable fatality.

The heavy aircraft lifted labouriously off the ground. Its wide wings cast shadows on receding fields. As we climbed into the sky, the concentric city came into full, magnificent view—the dome rose to the sky like a crystal mountain and elevated Selene, the keeper of our city, to divine status. Tunnels with metallic shells cut diagonally across the scarred landscape, connecting the five cities.

A storm was forming. Black, heavy clouds sat on the curved horizon. A thick, menacing atmosphere threatened to swallow heaven and earth. Dark volumes, morphed into shapes and faces, stories that spoke to those who dared look into the frightening mass, and it stole their sight to fuel its raging conquest. Lightning electrified the air as a deep rumble echoed moments later. The thunderstorms raged on.

PART TWO

NATURE

6

OUR RADARS were picking up heavy thunderstorms for miles ahead. Looking out the small, thick, airplane window, I saw giant clouds brooding as lightning lit up the sky. Eliah talked to the pilot.

"We will be fine," he said coming back and taking a seat beside me, "it seems there is a path through. We'll hit clear weather shortly after."

"Have you considered landing? We're over continental land. Maybe we can locate an old airstrip and wait it out."

"Nothing within vicinity. We're keeping our eyes open. An emergency landing will cost us our ride home and it's a long way home. We need to make it through! We're not far from the destination point."

He was apprehensive.

"It's a reinforced Antonov," a crew member said,

"a formidable machine. It takes more than that to take it down."

No one said a word. Everyone in the hull was tense, listening to every tremor, hoping that the storm would subside. Suddenly, the sky turned pitch black. The low vibration of the engines hummed through an eerie quiet. And then, the airplane went into heavy turbulence. The red emergency lights came on. A linguist among the crew, pulled an amulet out from beneath his shirt and muttered nervously. Selene couldn't help us out here. We rebelled against Her and attempted to overthrow Her kingdom. We had lost faith in another God a long time ago. The pilot spoke over the intercom.

"Captain coming in. Everyone buckle-up and hold tight. The storm has changed trajectory. We are enclosed on all sides. Going right through … Pray if you believe in something Greater. Over."

I leaned forward and saw the co-pilot close the cockpit door. I sensed his fear. Eliah grabbed my arm.

"We will make it. We must!"

The plane shook violently. Ice and hail hit the hull and thick plastic windows. An immense force rocked the aircraft and I quickly lost confidence in the heavily-reinforced carrier. I tightened my harness and helmet buckle. My stomach churned as we descended sharply.

Bang, bang, bang.

Desperate faces looked at each other. A soldier smiled … at Death itself. The linguist sweated profusely, rapidly repeating words of prayer.

Pray if you believe in something Greater.

Not fear of death but longing and regret filled my heart. When we parted, I never said goodbye. You hid your tears as I left. I should have stayed and kept you in my embrace. I yearned to see you again.

A flame flared up in the darkness outside as one of the engines caught fire. A dull explosion was followed by the sound of bending steel. The wind whistled relentlessly. The aircraft leaned sharply. I looked at Eliah—he didn't say a word, defiantly facing the unfolding tragedy, unwilling to accept the inevitable. His defiance turned into utter disbelief as the aircraft's immense wing ruptured.

"Noooo!"

Eliah screamed bestially.

"No! No! No!"

His last expression of defiance, his unshakable belief that he could bend reality to his will, was meaningless. The aircraft fell uncontrollably from the sky. The hull split open and one by one we were pulled into the storm's vortex—lost souls. Screams were swallowed by the rage of howling winds. I was pulled into a night as dark as tar, falling through a maelstrom, a devilish whirlpool of violent forces. Like disgraced angels with broken wings, we fell from heaven unto Earth. Heavy bodies hit damp soil in dull thuds—it was our requiem. Thunderstorms on the horizon moved ever so slow, ravaging Earth, repenting humanity's sins.

• • •

In a realm between reality and dream, spirits and ghosts rose out of ashen soil to conjure souls, and guide them to the netherworld. Their expressions were carved by grey smoke and a shifting wind breeze. They were spirits from centuries ago, or vague memories from deep recesses of mind. Gathered with outstretched arms, they leaned in to touch the deceased with cold fingertips.

Nebulous, like the residue of an old photograph, I saw grandfather with the empathetic features I remembered him by. He reached out his large, emaciated hand, and whispered in my ear.

Come with us, child.

The other ghosts repeated the same silent words—an invitation to the other side. My soul shook loose, but was still attached to this world, held by a thin, silken thread tied securely around the heart. The ghosts waited. They could wait for centuries on end as if minutes were passing—dispersed data of this world, memories forever caught in an ether between time and space, living beyond the tides of time into eternity.

"Not yet," I said faintly, holding on to life.

They urged me on. I was on a threshold, a step away from another world. But they left, like reluctant guests in the afterhours of a banquet honoring the dead. One by one, they vanished into the smoke, fading back into the ashen earth. Faint whispers pleaded with the wind.

A burning field stretched into the far distance. Within the flames I saw the fleeting moments of my life. In the middle of the field knelt a woman, cloaked in white velvet. She held an infant. I recognized the green eyes—it was you. You reached out and offered the infant imploringly, the one we had been waiting for all these years. The fire separated us, and it turned into an endless crystal dome— the city of lost dreams. Grey ash rose from the ground and filled the air as if it were snowing. You searched for a way out—a gate, or a crack in the crystal so that your voice could travel and I could hear you speak. Yet, the dome was impenetrable. Its smooth, polished surface captured you. You hit the glass walls, screaming as the infant cried. Enclosed in the half-sphere, your voice was inaudible. Your hands bled, and the blood ran into the white sleeves of the velvet cloak until it was soaked in red. You fell to the ground, giving up on reaching me, and caressed the crying infant at your bosom. Red flowers blossomed out of the blood-stained cloak and fell to your feet. The child calmed as you held it—the mother of nativity. The kings were on their way, a star guided their way. I said your name. My voice was faint—a breath, a rustle of leaves in the autumn wind, a lullaby at full moon submerged in the breaking waves of an open ocean. The ocean, it came crashing, drowning us in its bottomless depths. Then it subsided. You were gone.

A lone survivor, a damned soul, or else, a prince of the underworld watching over his infernal realm. Debris was scattered as far as the eye could see. A putrid smell of burned flesh and waste thickened the air. Petroleum--soaked trees caught fire. At the far end of the world, I was helpless and lost.

Pain assured me that I was still alive. Struggling to breathe, I unfastened the harness and collapsed onto hot mud—gasping for air, groaning, inch by inch crawling towards a clearing in the burning forest to escape the flames. Ever-strong whispers haunted me from the bowels of the earth, invisible hands pulled from deep beneath the soil.

Come with us.

The words rose like haze.

With great effort I escaped the burning inferno of the crash site to a forest clearing where the air was cool and the damp soil felt soothing. Dew on wild grass, brushed against my forehead.

A flock of crows circled above the trees, hoarsely croaking messages from the netherworld. Sensing my weakness, they circled lower and landed nearby, beating their black wings against my battered body, pecking with sharp, oily beaks. I was defenseless against them. It was then when a large falcon with pointed wings dove from the sky and snatched one of the black-plumed birds. The falcon's sharp claws dug into the blue flesh of the crow and an avian battle unfolded as the other birds chased the majestic predator. Swarmed and slowed by the weight of its prey, the falcon escaped only with difficulty high above the clouds, emitting a victorious cry. Bewildered, the other crows settled in a barren tree, hesitant to fly again.

The sky opened with heavy rainfall. An outcrop on the periphery of the forest glade had a recess in its rock face, a cavern deep enough to provide shelter from the elements. Despite the rain, the approaching night glowed with petroleum-fueled, incandescent light. I listened to water drip on stone and run off along thin crevices to collect in small pools or seep through clay ground. Heavy trees fell under their own weight as their trunks smouldered and turned to charcoal in the wet forest. Night descended and brought uncertainty with it.

Ahna.

I said your name—it was my prayer.

Apparitions weaved into restless dreams. The ghosts cried and tried to break free out of stone walls, morphing into ancient charcoal drawings, tracing enigmatic geometries. The wind howled. Rain fell heavily on charred soil and washed away the silent wails of wingless men. Shadows shifted shape into forms resembling visions that I was afraid to see.

A noise, a moment of hesitation, heavy breath, damp footsteps on muddy soil. Out of the night, from behind the rain curtain, appeared a tall silhouette. In the dark, I couldn't discern the visitor—a survivor or a wild beast of the forest? The shadow approached with a cautious gait.

"Who are you?" I said, frightened.

The tall shadow crouched silently. Then I saw the sharp claws that dug into the clay ground, large feathered wings wrapped around the shadow like a cloak. I recognized it— the falcon with its notched beak. Its predatory gaze had a vigilant calm that watched over me in a sort of trance or meditation. It whistled a quiet melody. The melody seemed familiar, resurfacing through forgotten memories. In vain I tried to remember, as if my life depended on the recollection. But the hum comforted and healed, rising through the fog of time. The anthropomorphic shadow inhaled and exhaled strength that flowed through my constricted veins. With every breath, it rose and grew taller until it filled the whole of the cavern, its wings spread out and circumscribed the walls. I looked with deference at the metamorphosis that unfolded somewhere in a realm between reality and dream. Gently, the night air kindled like incense in a sacred ritual as the falcon stoked the smoke with its enormous wings, dissolving the charcoal figurines of ghosts.

Go on.

Unspoken words rose through the notes of the melody. The soft hum was like a faint trace, a bread crumb on a trail of an enchanted forest. A peace of mind set in, and with it, strength to confront the unknown, and ultimately death itself. A resolute certainty gripped me that all my life led up to this moment and all to come hereafter. The falcon held me with protective caress, far away from home—the crystal city. It was only the other night that, by your side, I kissed you. You could have been home by now, waiting in our garden where we spend summer days building dreams together. Now you were a dream I longed to return to.

Alone in an unforgiving wilderness that claimed the lives of my compatriots; alone in a silent dialogue with the anthropomorphic shadow that blended with the night, and slowly seeped back into the rock, disappearing into the crevasses of the hollow cave. It was a shadow and nothing more. Then, it was no more. I fell asleep under the heavy blanket of a starless sky. A dim sunrise meekly trickled on limestone walls glazed by rainwater. A vague recollection of a dream. Against all odds, I had survived.

• • •

The fires had dwindled but smoke still rose from the burned ground of the crash site. Cold air sat densely in the forest glade. Morning dew weighted heavily on tall grass that swayed in a gust of wind. Winter songbirds joined a daybreak chorus and black crows croaked hoarsely. Wild beasts grunted in the foliage of thorny shrubs. Insects from the microcosm of the forest chirped noisily.

A sound mosaic filled the dawn. The forest breathed. I heard the wilderness that was: still, complete, harsh, and unforgiving. I heard it all—the human silence.

Rainwater soaked the ground and flowed into calcite caves beneath, then found its way into a stream, a river, and then the sea, to rise into the sky, and fall again to earth. Clouds dropped onto the forest canopy like silken mountains in lush valleys. The forest, the earth, and everything on it seemed to move in a slow perpetual motion, pulling the sky along in a reversed kinetic process. The sky was anchored to the universe beyond like a ship moored in a bay of a vast inflowing ocean—steady, buoyant in cosmic tidal waves that were ever flowing at the speed of light.

Go on.

A wave of sudden pain shot through all fibres of my nervous system. Screaming in agony, I was startled by the harshness of my own voice that reverberated off the stone walls. Ghosts still hid behind those walls, enticing me to rest. And if I were to stay, would I dream, fall asleep never to awaken again? Or was there nothing at all—a molecular decomposition, a chemical dissolution of self—a life lost, meaningless in its own creation? The cavern enclosed me like a womb. First, it sheltered and protected, now the walls caved in. I crawled out to breath, to be born again after encountering Death itself.

The crashed aircraft was behind evergreen firs that had burned barren but stood firmly rooted on the periphery of the field. Torn metal pierced the ground like alloy flora.

"Hello! Is anyone out there?"

I shouted, disheartened.

Echoes and silence. I roamed from one end to another, scavenging for what remained, but there was nothing, only ashen soil. I realized that I had to keep going east. We were close to our destination before coming down in the storm. If the Losts existed, they were my only hope. They might have seen the falling plane, the fire in the forest. And I was afraid to spend another night out here, afraid of visions and ghosts that would take my soul away. So, I left deep into the forest to search for a hearsay people.

• • •

For days on end I stumbled deeper into an endless green labyrinth, with no East from where the sun rose, and no West to where it set—the forest was monotonous in its multitude of expressions. I fell, crawled, and stood up, holding on to entwined roots that broke through the earth like long tentacles of terrifying monsters. The monsters struggled to free themselves from a subterranean realm. And when they surfaced, they could not see the wonders surrounding them, for they were blind, living centuries below the ground. They did not see the colours of this world and crawled back into the dense soil, leaving their tentacles exposed to claim the conquest of the Earthly realm.

"Keep going a little longer," I told myself, "… until the tree over there, that rock further out, until I find a stream with water to drink."

But the forest had no end. There was no home on the other side of the wilderness, only a vague, fading hope of finding a lost people.

At night, when the sky was clear, the moon cast eerie shadows, revealing hidden spirits, in a pale blue light. Stars shone with a bright splendour—every time a shooting star fell, I whispered your name with a promise to come home again.

I love you.

I pictured myself saying in your ear, remembering how we used to stay up all night, keeping each other warm, and inventing stories of other worlds, of lovers looking back at us from distant solar system that circled an extinguished star. We were a million years apart. With thoughts of you, I surrendered to the forest, the sacred house of God.

The hidden symmetry of Nature was determined by pure chance. Centuries old trees with crowns entangled in the canopies of others, formed impenetrable archways, like pillars of a green cathedral, where even light did not pass through. Green and wet, earthy brown with splashes of poisonous colours; tints and hues, snakes, toads and stinging flowers, bats and birds—all life forms fought for survival, hunting, praying, and scavenging, only to be prayed on by others. Life circled nature's multiplicity of mad expressions. The forest breathed a heavy sigh to exhale and inhale its own creation, growing in new genetic permutations. Passing autumn and coming winter, some flowers bloomed when the icy rain fell, while others shed their leaves unto cold ground. The soil nourished seeds that awaited the next spring to sprout according to blueprints of their molecular arrangement. Nature lived in a rhythm of its own accord, beautiful in its violent composition. I wandered on, a deteriorating body and a mind losing cohesion, wild eyes stared out of hiding places.

"Come out!" I shouted.

There was no one.

At last, close by, I heard water flowing—the woods cleared unto a riverbank. Exhausted, starving and in pain, I dragged myself across coarse pebble and submerged my face in water. Ghosts looked back at me from the bottom of the riverbed and I saw myself sink like a heavy stone resigned to fate. Violently, I reemerged and gasped for air, before collapsing in the last throes of life.

How fragile life was—a fleeting moment torturing us with the promise of things to come until it was all over. Our illusion of permanence fell to earth that we stood so firmly on, or so we thought, as dust. And then it went on. Or it was just there, while we were left behind with hope that the memory of us would live on, that someone would utter our name in the future and through their words bring us back to life. But all that was left were faint echoes.

Sunlight reflected off the river in kaleidoscopic patterns. The flowing water shimmered in the late autumn light and shrouded the landscape in prismatic colours. The trees and rocks, the sky above, the earth, the river, all blended into a magnificent mosaic that flooded the world with a tender luminosity. Like reversed waves folding on their crest, geometries converged centerfold. I extended my hand towards the centre of symmetry and felt an inner warmth. Holding on to empty space, I exhaled deeply.

A man lay on a riverbank, out in a vast wilderness where no other man was thought to be, far away from home. The wind nursed him as the river flowed through his chafed hands, cleansing his wounds. Emaciated, dry foam crust the corners of his starving mouth. Black birds circled in the sky to offer him to the spirits of the wild. Suddenly, people appeared out of the deep forest. Smeared in clay and mud, blending with the grey landscape, they were Earthen-people. Carefully, they approached the man lying by the river who was like them yet, different. They turned his unresponsive body with long sticks. The man was breathing faintly and still alive. One pressed the sharpened end of his spear against the man's heart and asked in a deep hoarse voice, a language from the past:

"Kill?"

"No. Take him to Father," said another one.

7

Hastily the Earthen-people build a makeshift raft of logs and branches held together by bark fiber, and secured the stranger onto it. A mountainous Earthen-man harnessed the contraption on his strong shoulders and, thus, off they went downriver, traversing Nature's dangerous frontier. Only the fool-hearted once believed that they could own Her, but Nature, a generous hostess, always remained enduring.

They travelled along rugged terrain and stayed the watercourse. The wild river wound violently to a waterfall that fell into a pool, diverging in multitude of streams that reunited once again with distant rivers and the sea. The Earthen-people entered the deep woods once again and navigated with ease the dense thickets that were an impassable fortress to those who didn't know their way.

They traveled day in, day out and through the nights. Like migrating birds that fled winter to unknown places south across the sea, the Earthen-people too were weary of the winter to come. Some of them would not survive this one—they knew as much. Returning from their last foray into the forest, they carried game, fowl and boar, on their strong backs. They traveled fast with hope to reach their kin before long.

On their way across the woods, straight lines and right angles emerged on moss covered ground. The passage eased. An old, paved road revealed itself from beneath algae growing through the stone. Reverent of the place, the travelers stopped to lay wreath of flowers and burn sage; they sacrificed a fowl to share among themselves, and offered the best cuts to appease the spirits of the road, that they may grant safe passage through what lay before.

The road led through a desolate city—weathered by centuries of corrosive forces, monolithic shapes stood veiled by green flora; steel and stone towers marveled at their own decayed splendour like shrines to an old world. Tree roots broke through concrete foundations and weaved up vertical walls like dragons swallowing their tail. The Earthen-people entered the tall, ancient city that shielded the sky from rain falling in bursts of violent downpour, and turned day into night by absorbing daylight in its vertical density. The travelers lit their torches and made their way into the haunted forest city that bathed their faces in a green hue.

"Let us rest," said an Earthen-man.

They found recluse in a stone tower that extended far into the forest like an infinitely rising mountain, some sort of temple, surely a place of worship to an unknown, powerful God. Through a maze of chambers they settled in the tower's heart—a high atrium with twisting, overgrown walls where birds had nested. They gathered around a campfire to share a meal and rest for the night. A young Earthen-man prepared an herbal brew for the injured stranger and applied ointment of ground antiseptic leaves to his bruised body. In harmony, the Earthen-people whistled a melody quietly into the night, a song of love and sorrow that filled the stranger's heart. They never spoke a word.

I burned with fever and shivered with cold tremors underneath layers of warm pelts. The bitter brew, a medicine of the forest, dispersed its compounds through my system, and took hold of it. Geometries and patterns began to form in the campfire. In the shadows cast by the flames, I saw a silken cocoon, nested between the twisting walls—a giant, nocturnal moth was maturing. Terrified, I pointed at it frantically, but the Earthen-people slept already. Only the young one, the medicine-man, came to reassure me, putting a wet cloth on my burning forehead.

"Lie still," he said soothingly, "sleep."

I could not take my eyes off the giant moth.

"Sleep," the young Earthen-man repeated.

He put his rough hand over my eyes and then left me be.

The moth awoke. It moved, broke free, tearing the elastic silk from within the cocoon shell. The brittle web burst and a new life appeared—monstrous and colossal. Liberated, the moth beat its wings a thousand beats per minute as wavelengths of its movement flowed through the night air. It ascended and floated in the high vault of the ancient tower. Its colours, reminiscent of the surrounding night, tarnished it from the predators of midnight. Allured by the campfire light, it descended lower to the flames, before its wings caught fire. It stayed afloat and let out a piercing cry, setting the green overgrowth of the twisting walls aflame, until the whole tower was burning. Birds fled their nests and encircled the giant moth. Something stirred in my belly and I struggled to breath as if bile rose through my airways. A moth crawled out of my mouth, followed by another, and then hundreds of others. They swarmed out towards the monstrous, burning creature and all perished alike in the flames, turning to ash. The birds disappeared into the night. The Earthen-people were fast asleep, only the medicine-man watched carefully over me.

"Sleep," he repeated once again, "Tomorrow you will feel better."

He poured fresh water into a gourd and wet the cloth on my forehead. I fell into a dreamless sleep.

• • •

We travelled on through the ancient forest city. Our torches, lit at daytime, amplified dark hues of aged mono-liths. Wild animals roamed abandoned streets. I was of this world again—my body was weak but my mind whole again. I observed the Earthen-people as they navigated the terrain: sturdy with fair, grey skin and piercing eyes that shone in green and brown and bluish colours. Their eyes sat in deep eye-sockets and were smeared with black soot, frightening to the appearance. Their hair was long of a light ash colour, falling across broad foreheads and gaunt faces. Covered in pelts, crudely stitched leather, and salvaged fabrics, they carried long, sharpened sticks as weapons. The Earthen-people travelled without talking, only quietly whistling to one another. They were weary of this place's past, fearful of awakening the old spirits.

Another day and night had passed before we reached the woodland edge. The forest lifted its green veil and we stood at the shores of a dry seabed, haunted by an empty sea. The ancient city went on past the beaches along the scorched plateau that was like the dusty skin of a lizard, thick and flaking, with deep grooves between old leathery cells. Rust ate the steel structures and ceroplastic towers. Concrete walls were eroded by dust and wind. Sand dunes filled streets and alleys with crystal grains. Polished stone, like granite mirrors, reflected the night sky, and pulled stars towards the earth, housing them along long avenues, rationalizing infinity in decayed city blocks.

We travelled past giant ships with corroded hulls and exposed iron skeletons. Tilted on their curved bellies, they haven't seen the sea for centuries. They longed for the salty sea to bury them in its elemental force, to carry them off onto coral reefs so that they could meet their rightful end beneath foaming waves of restless waters. But it wasn't to be. Like stranded whales, colossal in their mass, they cried for receded waters, knowing full well that they would never see the sea again. The ships lamented their fate as the wind, in its never-ending journey, tore at their skin with granular force.

I asked the Earthen-people in a wordless conversation,
Where is the sea to where the rivers flow?
Listen.
They said pointing at the ground.

I put my ear to the dry seabed and listened carefully to what was below. Oh, could it be or was it just imagination? The wind howled above, far beneath the surface, ascending to the ground, the sound of waves rising, falling, flowing, and breaking on subterranean shores— a living sea deep below the dry seabed or a memory of a place—the sea that once was and, perhaps, would come back again, one day.

We left the ancient city, away from the old ruins inhabited by restless spirits, away from steel and stone monuments that stood forgotten in the shadows of a lost world. On the other side of the basin, we reached rocky shores at the foot of a mountain range. Seashells and old artifacts hid among rock formations that were submerged in the sea a long time ago.

The Earthen-people pulled me on a wooden raft overlaid by pine branches up into the mountains, through narrow passages with loose rocks beneath their feet. As we passed a hollow crevice along a tall ridge, the Earthen-people clicked their tongues in a rhythmic spell to ward off an evil spirit. I looked closely and saw a deceased man—a solitary recluse or, perhaps, a wanderer escaping the old seaside city, immortalized by the cold, dry mountains. Skeletal hands blackened by frost wrapped around his frozen body in a desperate attempt for warmth. Strands of white hair fell to the sides of his weathered face. Torn scraps of bright-coloured cloths flapped in the wind. He was like a centuries old guide cautioning of the road ahead, silently reminding passerby of the perils to come. Small bells strung across the crevice chimed in the wind. The Earthen-people cast their eyes away and chanted spells, fearful of the spirit that sat steadfast, mesmerized by a changed world.

We climbed higher into the mountains. At times, we could see the dry seabed far below. The ancient city punctured the vast plain and cast elongated shadows as the sun set behind rectangular geometries that framed the red and purple sky. Clouds touched the forest that swallowed the city at the narrow line of the horizon. Covered in pelts, we spend the night huddled close together, inhaling thin air, craving oxygen. Vertical plateaus rose towards the stars like mighty fortresses build by giants, overwhelming in size. Echoes in the valleys. Silence in the mountains. Only bells rang somewhere in the wind.

Frost bitten, the Earthen-people slept deeply. The dark night, crisp and clear, was faintly illuminated by stars that slowly faded into a white and blue morning. The Earthen-people awoke with wary minds. Honoring the night, deferent of the day to come, they rose all but one—one remained seated by the extinguished fire, the light had left his heart.

"Come back. Come back to us."

The Earthen-people waited for their brother to return, but his journey continued elsewhere. They laid him out on the frozen ground, just off the traveler's path, and stone by stone raised a burial mound—a marker for wayfarers to come. Their Earthen-brother was to become a silent storyteller of his time, telling of his people that wandered these forests and valleys—a people that had lost their world but had survived.

Once, caravans left the cities and passed these mountains. Now, none. The Earthen-people retraced the old roads and scavenge for what was left of the bygone world. Returning home, they ascended the windward mountain face to descend on the leeward side to safety. A river divided the black soil in low marshlands that, along the riparian, was lined by poplar trees. The landscape shifted between deep autumn hues and a monochrome winter. The Earthen-people were restless with subdued joy.

"We are here. Almost."

They cried into the dawn.

Streams of smoke rose in the distance.

"Come out," they said in quiet unison.

Wooden huts on stilts scattered along the riverbank. Crusted in mud and hands stained in soil, Earthen-people appeared in the pastel morning to welcome the home-comers. The travelers embraced their kin and restless children of the Earth that shed tears of joy and sang songs of sorrow to mourn a brother lost on the way. There were few of them—a people like no other, they rode the raging winds and moved with the ebb and flow of rivers. A people that carried a myth of a great past on tired shoulders, their lineage scattered among ruins of ancient cities like faded footsteps on sand swept away by tides, like shallow incisions on weathered rock, scars on million-year-old fossils.

The Earthen-people watched the stranger with reverence and fear, like a fateful messenger from a hearsay world that they only knew from their Father's tales. They also saw a broken man whose life hung by a thin thread. There was little to be done, for only the will to live assured life out here. Earthen-children hid behind mothers or played with woodcut figurines—half-beast, half-human—their world, unalterable in its harsh trajectory, was to be altered after all. A falcon flew by.

• • •

A hearth, inlaid on a clay floor and stones, burned in the middle of a hut. The mud walls were reinforced with lodge pole pines. Outside, I heard voices in a remnant language preserved from the past—words were whispered and sang so as not to disturb the wind. The hearth fire crackled as if fueled by a petroleum-soaked earth. With great dread I recalled the blast of engines and human cries lost in a storm.

Come with us.

An Earthen-man entered the hut. It was the young medicine-man that had tended to me on the journey through the ancient forest city and empty sea, through the mountains and into this valley. He sat by my side.

"My name is Yvan," he spoke in a deep voice pressing his hand against his chest.

I tried to answer but my mouth was dry and aching. I hadn't said a word in days, perhaps longer. He offered me water and waited patiently.

"Where are you from?"

Where was I from—a vague dream? You made the dream real, giving it a place, a name, somewhere to return to.

"Star City," I said at last with great effort and a strained voice.

"Star City?"

The Earthen-man was taken aback.

"Star City? Where is this place? All stars have fallen a long time ago."

"The other side of the sea."

"The Sea-That-Was? The Waterless-Sea?"

"The Sea-That-Is," I replied in his manner.

Yvan pondered in awe. For the Earthen-people the world had ended and started anew. Only ancient ruins and myths of once great people remained.

"I know of this sea. It is far away ... We have never crossed it. Have you? How?"

"Airplane," I gestured a flying motion with my hands, "have you seen one before?"

"I have never seen one. But I know of it. Father had told us."

"Father?"

"Father had told us many things. He remembers. An airplane is a giant iron bird."

Yvan paused to imagine these iron birds flapping their wings, commanding the sky. He thought of all the wonders of the old world that had brought man to the precipice of gods before everything perished, just when the greatest gift of all was within reach. Or so, the Earthen-people thought. Were there really others that had preserved the old, mythical knowledge?

"You came alone?"

"No," I said painfully.

"Where are the others?"

I remained silent but the young Earthen-man understood.

"They were your brothers and sisters."

His voice was filled with sadness and he touched his heart with an open palm in a gesture of shared sorrow. He felt the stranger's loss and longing, just as he felt it in his own people who longed for a place far away from these creeks, away from the tall poplar trees and wet marshes. His people held on to a story of a fabled place told to them as children, the story they tell their children now— it grew in their minds, taking on forms and colours, meaning of their own making, a reasons to endure the hardships of this world, for they would return home one day. And their home would be warm and plenty, with others like them waiting on their return.

Father said that someone would come one day and lead them back to the promised city. None ever came. Father hadn't spoken in years. Was the stranger the messenger they had been waiting for, or an orphan of the world, lost just like them? If Star City was real, the Earthen-people would find a way across the Great Sea. For them, this world was unbearable. Not so for Yvan. He didn't long for elsewhere, for he was free—Nature nurtured him, the wind was his brother that taught him many things when it howled and screamed, when it sat still in the valleys and whispered. Yvan belonged here. The others did not understand. How could he love this unforgiving world when there was another one—golden and precious? But all that Yvan saw was the beauty and might of Nature. All things returned to where they once came from, and we all came from the soil, the water in the rivers, the rain in the sky, the light of the burning sun, and the darkness of a moonless night. This is where it all started, and this is where it will all end.

"I have to return home."

"You have to heal first," Yvan replied in his soft demeanor.

"There is someone … ."

"We are far away."

Yvan washed my face and feet. He then broke off a chunk of crudely baked wild barley bread. The bread, hard and grainy, was precious to them.

"Rest."

He left the hut. Alone, I watched the flames on the hearth. Ghosts haunted me with pleading screams from the other side. In solitude, I always saw you.

• • •

A melody played in the background, the one I had heard so many times in my dreams before. Sweet fruit oil aroma pleasantly scented warm, humid air—it smelled like evening in a rainforest. Nightingales sang nearby. A light breeze softly brushed my perspiring body. I dreamt of a wondrous city with a crystal sky. Seasons changed through autumn, winter, spring, and summer. A pale moon lay so low that I reached up and touched it. It cracked wide open and revealed a blackness underneath that veiled the entire city.

A beautiful woman with bright, emerald eyes knelt by my side, grinding leaves in a mortar bowl. Her thick, black hair fell over broad, painted shoulders.

Mother.

The prince has awakened.

I dreamt of a crystal city.

You will meet Her there, the Moon Goddess.

Will I recognize Her?

I was walking down the Avenue of Gods playing a flute, a song that I had learned as a child. My mother would sing it before sleep to guide me into the world of dreams, a world so easily forgotten with each sunrise. Now, this song was to carry me to heaven never to be forgotten again. Darkness was to turn into eternal light if I only remembered Her name. So, the elders said.

Remember Her name.

A crowd had gathered. They watched, talked, and reached out to me. I had prepared for this my whole life. Now that the moment was near, I was to grasp eternal light and never let it go again to be joined among stars— every journey led back home again.

She broke free from the crowd and fell on her knees, kissing my feet.

Don't go.

We can be together.

Ahna, my love, don't lure me back into your embrace.

The Moon Goddess has promised eternal life.

She was lost again.

With every step taking you closer to your end, do you plead to stay alive, or fight to survive like a man drowning in a strong current? Do you walk with joy approaching paradise? It all depends what you expect to find on the other side. It all depends if you're willing to leave everything behind. Oh, sweet melody, you fill my heart with strength. Where others would falter with fear, doubt in their minds, I walked on steadily.

I ascended the Tower of a Thousand Steps. The crowd drew further back with each upward tread. I was in a trance. Step, step, step, and one last step. The elders were waiting, bloodthirsty. I knew the ritual. I had seen it before. I had prepared for it. I played the last note and broke the flute, throwing the pieces into a burning pit. The melody remained to guide me. A broken flute—transient lives. Everything comes to an end. The ritual began.

Weepers danced in a slow rhythm, eyes rolled back in ecstasy, pleading with ancient Gods for salvation.

Fix your mind on the stars and you will be given a place among them.

So, the elders said.

Selene give me wisdom.

Give me eternal life.

I lay down on the stone altar stained red with old sacrifices, my chest bared to the Moon above. The elders prayed in unison, their faces hidden behind spirit masks with terrifying expressions. The weepers danced in a bloodcurdling flow. The elders rubbed cremation ash onto my torso and face, supplicating the Moon Goddess for mercy and acceptance.

Remember Her name.

The Moon shone bright in the night sky as the priest raised the sacrificial dagger. Your voice echoed from down below.

Come back.

Ahna.

In the moment of transcendence, I longed for you. The elders offered my bleeding heart to the Moon. Dark clouds swept across the sky and hid the moonlight. The weepers wailed and prayed, chanting louder. The elders burned my heart in a sacred chalice in a last effort at redemption. The sky closed with heavy clouds—a thunderstorm was forming. I fell from the Tower of a Thousand Steps back onto Earth. A long journey to find you again awaited me.

The dreams I dreamt. I never used to dream, only the images televised by dreamcatchers into our subconscious that Selene imbued with hope, devotion, and belief, molding our reality to Her arithmetic whims. She suppressed our nightmares with bright lights in an artificial world to fill our minds with forced optimism. Our psyche was clinically enlightened where no dark corners nor uncertainties remained. There was no room for doubt, only the promise of prosperity lay ahead. That much was certain, She owned our dreams, sterilizing our reality. But out here, Star City was just a small, translucent pearl hidden beneath a green and foaming ocean. All the suppressed fears and nightmares—images and sounds, past lives and parallel realities—burst forth through buried memories. I had lived this life a million times over. Eliah was right, what was left of us but a deep urge to feel—love, joy, pain, and sorrow. I gave up transcendence to be with you. I dreamed of your warmth, the rhythm of your heart, the sound of your voice. I had to return to you.

The fire in the hearth had died down. However, daylight shone weakly through cracks in the mud walls. Shortly after I awoke, Yvan walked in.

"Awake?" he asked quietly.

"Yes," a foul taste in my mouth, "how long did I sleep?"

"A day and a night."

He refilled the drinking gourd with fresh water. I gulped it down. It cleared my head and soothed my burning belly.

"In your sleep you repeated a name, Ahna."

"I have to return to her," I said weakly.

Yvan didn't answer but tended to the swellings on my

body, applying ointment brewed from the forest flora.

"Tonight, we will feast and honor the stranger from Star City. All brothers and sisters will attend. Father will attend. The feast will begin soon."

I nodded.

He left again. I tried to recall the dream and its violent impressions—I had made a great sacrificed to be with you; once again, I will sacrifice to return to you. It was inevitable. Whatever was to come, I was ready.

• • •

The Earthen-people carried me under the stars of the Milky Way that shone with a silken glow. I remembered the halls of the Zodiac that, in a ludicrous attempt, simulated the infinite depth of star systems on flat plastic ceilings. Silhouettes of Earthen-people formed a path to a fire lit ground that was ceremoniously laid out with gifts and offerings; wild meats roasted on a bonfire. They all gathered round. Father sat wordlessly at the center, wrapped in thick pelts and woven gowns. Like an old oak tree, hollow in its core, deep roots anchored him to the ground—he held on to life. Blessed by his presence, the Earthen-people greeted him by kissing his feet. They looked into his blind eyes, whispered into his deaf ears as the old man sat in resolute silence. Yvan, the young medicine-man, stepped forward to open the ceremony.

"My brothers and sisters, we are here tonight to honour the stranger. Father bless us."

"Father bless us," the Earthen-people repeated all together.

"We found the stranger beyond the Sea-That-Was, the Waterless-Sea," Yvan continued, "beyond the ancient city. We found the stranger by a river. He says that he fell from the sky, from the belly of a mighty, iron bird."

Surprise and disbelief arose among the gathered.

"The stranger tells lies," hoarse voices spoke out from the crowd, "iron birds flew a long time ago."

"The stranger says that he had crossed the Great Sea, the Sea-That-Is, the Plentiful Sea."

"What lies beyond the Great Sea? If stranger had crossed it, he must know."

"City," Yvan responded.

The Earthen-people were mistrustful of the stranger's tale.

"There are cities before the Great Sea. There must be cities after it. But they are empty cities, inhabited by spirits from the past. They are cities of the dead."

Many agreed.

"Stranger says that there is a city of the living, Star City."

"All cities have fallen," said the hoarse voices.

"The stranger knows of things that only Father knows of and father hasn't spoken in many years."

"The stranger is just like us. He heard tales from our ancestors."

"Father said that one day a saviour will come and show us the way to a City of Stars," said some.

"We searched for many years and we crossed many rivers, mountains, valleys, and forests. But we never saw a city of the living. We never found a City of Stars," replied others.

"The stranger must come from somewhere."

"The stranger comes from nowhere. He fell from the sky," the hoarse voices said mockingly.

And so, the Earthen-people argued—some wanted to believe that the stranger would guide them to another world, away from hardships; others saw a broken man from an unbeknownst place.

"Let the stranger speak. He speaks a language like ours," Yvan said finally.

All fell quiet.

"Speak my friend," Yvan encouraged me.

I hesitated.

"He is a mute but can fly like a bird!" the hoarse voices broke the quiet as laughter erupted.

"It is true. There are cities, Cities of Stars on the other side of the Great Sea," I finally brought myself to speak through the laughter and noise.

The Earthen-people became so quiet again that only the crackling fire, the forest, and the creek nearby was heard.

"Go on stranger. Speak," said the hoarse voices.

"There are five cities. I come from the city of the Moon, Star City Selene ... ."

I told them about Selene at the heart of our Confederates nurturing Her children, Her digital consciousness resting in a milky white chariot. She was the Mother Spirit the Earthen-people said. I told them about the Zodiac and the dome that enclosed it. I told them about Starsonians and how after many years of toil, they had reached prosperity and abundance. I told them as much as I could muster strength to tell, and it all seemed like magic to the Earthen-people, their minds were drunk with wonder. However, the hoarse voices were still doubtful.

"The stranger tells great tales. The world has ended. We were born again. Like children we must learn anew."

"We believe him," some said in my defense.

"The stranger has a good heart."

"Even a good heart can lead astray."

"This much is true."

"Let Father judge," Yvan said with heightened intuition.

He turned to the old man who sat motionless, his frail body hidden beneath thick pelts. The Earthen-people were surprised as Father hasn't spoken in many years.

"Father bless us," Yvan thus addressed the old man.

"Father bless us," repeated all the others.

The old man seemed lifeless.

"Father bless us. Father …" Yvan pleaded for the old man's blessing.

To everyone's great astonishment, the old man sighed deeply. The Earthen-people gasped and cried, prostrating at the feet of their venerated father. The old man's deep sigh was followed by prolonged silence that the Earthen- -people bore with pious patience. Then, after all these years, Father spoke.

"I have seen this man in my dreams," he said in the old language, with a barely audible voice, "he cometh from the City of Stars."

His blind, clairvoyant eyes searched for the stranger.

"Beware the starlight."

These were the last words he ever spoke.

"Father, we honor you," the Earthen-people said in an electrifying rush.

They kissed his feet, touched his rough gown, and howled wild cries into the night, breaking into an ecstatic dance.

"Beware the starlight? We yearn for it!"

"We know a way across the Great Sea. We must travel north where the waters freeze in winter. The journey is long and arduous, but we know a way. The stranger must promise that we will find the City of Stars on the other side of the Great Sea."

"I promise," I said longing for you.

"Then we will go," said determined Earthen-voices.

"We must find the City of Stars."

Hope of seeing you filled my heart. Little did I know that the journey I was bound on was of an entirely different nature. I was to die many times over to truly find you again.

The feast started. Earthen-women shared food of wild grains and roots, fruits harvested from the forests, hard bread and wild meat. Creek water fermented with berries was poured into wooden cups. Meager in their circumstance, the Earthen-people, were generous in their way. They danced and sang ballads of a lost world. Entranced by sorrow, they told stories of a once great kingdom ruled by kings and queens blinded by false riches. Red elixir seeped through their hands as they shouted—More! More! Give us more!—inciting violence and crime as sons and daughters sacrificed their lives for vain glory. Nature revolted and unleashed storms that ravaged the blue planet, burning the sky and flooding the Earth. Misguided souls fled steel and stone fortresses into forests and valleys. The Earthen-people danced with eyes fixed on stars. They prayed for redemption. Yet, the stars they dreamt of had long lost their luster and their warmth. The Earthen--people were rooted in the wet soil and it was there that they would meet their end. I was to cross another sea.

8

THE FOREST slept in the early hours of dawn, in-between when the night had passed but day had yet to arrive. A mist veiled meek morning light with molecular density. Dull echoes traveled through sparse trees that clung to acidic soil beneath high water tables. Insects sat in stagnant, algae covered ponds. Toads slumbered on white and blue water lilies. Young water spirits played a lazy game of hide-and-seek as the old ones watched, reminiscing about their bygone youth.

Dawn was disturbed by an Earthen-boy running—his hurried steps send tremors through water pools and frightened the young spirits. The older spirits, bothered by the untimely disturbance, slipped beneath the water surface. The boy breathed heavily as thick, cold air filled his laboring lungs. He had secretly gone to catch fireflies in the marshes. His brothers had forbidden him to go alone as there were many dangers lurking in the forest and marshes at night. But he often snuck out, curious about the glowing insects.

He hurried home with great haste. Startled and unsure of the things he had just seen: an apparition from the tales his brothers told to frighten him. Did his eyes and ears play a trick on him? Yet, he heard the murmur, smelled the burned grass, and saw the fast-moving star descend from the sky, growing larger, glowing in a spectrum of pulsing colours. The Earthen-boy hid in shrubs by the marshes and watched the bright star turn night into day, scattering the fireflies and scaring away nocturnal animals. The small boy recognized the mythical bird with iron wings from the ancient world. It didn't have feathers and sharp claws as he had always imagined, yet the turbulence of its powerful wings swayed the trees. A heat wave burned his skin as the bright bird landed softly on the marshland. It sat there breathing in the cold dawn air, breathing out hot condensed steam. The boy watched with awe, hypnotized by the iron bird's magnificence.

From within its belly appeared tall angels clad in white armour. They moved with heavy steps that sank into the soil. Purple crosses were painted on their plated chests. They wore gold cloaks that morphed colours. Their faces were hidden behind iron masks with eyes that shone in an electric light, scanning their surroundings like predatory animals, weapons in hand. The boy thought that one of the unearthly beings seemed to have noticed him, and he crawled deeper into the woods. Filled with terror, he ran away as fast as his legs would carry him to tell his brothers of all that he had seen. Dawn fully broke when the Earthen-boy reached home.

An anxious excitement filled the morning as the Earthen-people had by now all heard of the boy's encounter. I lay awake listening to the commotion outside when Yvan came in.

"What's going on?"

"They are here," Yvan said with a measured voice.

I understood at once. An amplitude of emotions tore at me, most of all a terrible foreboding of an impending fatality.

"Just like you, they crossed the Great Sea, the Plentiful Sea."

He told the Earthen-boy's story.

"Iron-clad angels have arrived in the belly of a mighty bird. They held swords and wore armour with purple crosses and gold cloaks. So, the boy said."

I was afraid, and Yvan felt my fear. The clergy found us. I wanted to believe that they came to take me back to Star City, back to you. But I knew that the cloaked priests had send their henchmen. They were here now.

"My friend, the angels from across the Great Sea are not here for peace but for destruction," I said with a heavy heart.

How could I explain the evil that had crept into the paradise we had built? How could I explain that the Goddess that we worshipped had flaws like any other? We could never escape our shadow—it was always there in each of us. We lit a fire and, as long as it burned, the shadow receded into peripheral corners of our minds. As soon as we neglected the fire, it emerged again to entice us with a seductive voice of power and immortality.

Yvan, the young medicine-man, looked at me with sorrow. He understood human nature with a pure wisdom. He saw all of it—the greatness and folly—in the stone and steel monuments of the old forgotten cities. Restless ghosts carved vague memories into brittle concrete. She was just another god among other, for paradise could exist only within. The paradise without would always remain a dream.

· · ·

"It smells like death."

"What does death smell like?"

"I imagine like this."

"We must warn the others."

He put a finger to his lips and then pointed outside.

"Listen."

Heavy, robotic footsteps, a burnt smell, the sound of flames tearing through air, then oppressive silence.

"They are here."

Ghosts crawled from beneath the ground and through the walls.

Come with us.

It is time.

Whispers and echoes.

"Run Yvan! You must escape!"

Yvan opened a floor hatch in the far corner of the hut that I hadn't noticed previously. He must have entered through it whenever he appeared as if out of nowhere. It connected to a tunnel that linked all the huts underneath the soil, and ended deep in the forest—a refuge for when storms came to this mountain side. He turned to help me.

"Go," I searched for courage in my heart, "save your-self! We won't make it together. You can on your own."

He hesitated. But he knew the laws of Nature—it honoured life and death with equal reverence.

"Run before it's too late!"

Black smoke seeped through the door seams. I poured water on a cloth and covered my nose and mouth.

"When the time comes, remember Her name."

Yvan foresaw the journey ahead of me. His own journey would be long and arduous if he were to escape the clergy's angels of destruction. He was the last of his kind. His kin lay in ashes on a cold winter's day, executed by the soulless messengers cloaked in golden robes, purple crosses on their armoured chests. The Earthen-people were forever lost in time. Yvan disappeared through the hatch.

I pray for you.

Smoke filled the hut as I gasped for air. Ghosts crowded around the fire that flared with oxidized flames. The door broke open and razor sharp light beams cut through the thick air, scanning the space. They entered in heavy iron suits, the clergy's henchmen, breathing through respirators, their faces hidden behind masks. They held burning swords in their hands. The light beams converged on me. I couldn't be sure if these were men or something different altogether. One of them stepped forward and pressed the hot blade against my chest. Ghosts whispered in the dense, oxygen deprived hut.

It is time.

"I am a citizen of Star City," I said coughing.

The iron-clad messenger paused to scan my face, locating my profile in a database uploaded to hissynthetic brain.

"You have betrayed Her Supreme Consciousness," he said in an artificial voice amplified by the mechanical breath of the respirator.

"Traitors of the City Confederates are punished with immediate death."

The half-human proclaimed justice of a constructed morality.

"On behalf of Selene and Her faithful servants, I, Commander of the Selenite Knights, protectors of the Confederates, serve you your sentence in accordance with the written code."

He pierced my heart with the burning blade. It burst in one painful moment.

Ahna, I will return to you.

• • •

Peace. Barefoot I stood in the torched hut and watched my reclined body. Thin, silken threads like invisible cobwebs fell off my hands, my eyes, my heart, and dissolved into the soil. I walked out into the cold and past the gold cloaked clerics. I heard them talk with delayed voices like distant echoes. Light vanished into the purple crosses on their iron plated chests, drawn into the abyss of their empty hearts. I saw their stone-carved faces behind the masks.

The soil was blackened by the ash of the Earthen--people. Scattered spirits hovered above deceased bodies, quietly mourning their lost selves. Ghosts laughed silently. Water in the creek nurtured the earth with a silver shine. The forest, with its old wisdom, sheltered life. The world shimmered in shadows and light. I rose towards the sky. From afar I saw an Earthen-man running through the wilderness. His stride was assured, his destiny determined. He carried knowledge in his heart and sorrow in his mind.

Farewell Yvan.

May the spirits guide you.

I saw Star City's aircraft on the marshlands. It lifted off, bending the forest with the force of its recoil, and flew off towards the Great Sea on the far horizon beyond the mountains, valleys, and abandoned cities. A storm formed at sea, blackening the sky, swallowing the aircraft in thunder. I rose into the dark sky and saw other sparks of light rising with me—lost souls of this world returned to their source.

PART THREE

SKY

9

ECHOES of a faraway wind. Echoes of unseen voices. Faint footsteps. I walked in darkness, treading on water. An endless tunnel morphed into voids, revealing places from the life I lived. Forgotten memories—birth, childhood, my adolescent years. I saw Star City, the shape of it. I saw my life go by in a fleeting instant.

Ghosts rose out of water and lined along the tunnel walls. Some were still, at peace, wishing well as I passed by. Others cried and screamed, vying for attention—broken promises, lost friends and lovers, unpaid debts, hurt souls, and vengeful words. They tore at my conscience, pulling me into the entangled voids of unresolved recollections.

Walk on steadily.

I heard a voice.

That life has passed.

I wavered with regret, desire, neglected dreams. My feet sank deeper with every step I took.

Knee deep.

Waist deep.

Chest deep.

I bore my sins and the memories forged by them like heavy rocks, like a million grains of sand that weighed me down, dragging me below the water surface. I had to vindicate myself.

Chin deep.

I struggled to breath.

Let go.

That voice again.

This life has passed.

Life is an expression.

A thought.

Go on.

I lived my life the way I knew how to live. Memories are thoughts, my sins—desires.

Cast the stones aside.

The water receded and I breathed again as the ghosts merged into the tunnel walls wailing and laughing. The tunnel ascended to a light that brightened the darkness and embraced me with a soothing warmth.

• • •

A white desert beneath a crimson red sky by the shores of a black ocean. My bare feet dug into hot desert sand. The black water washed away my footsteps as I walked along the shoreline. An electric thunder hit the ocean that extended into a curved infinity. White sand dunes shifted shape. The wind crossed the barren landscape.

On the fading desert horizon appeared a mirage of an elephant-headed Deity, a sleepwalker in a dream. The giant Deity's tusks pierced the sky. He towered like a tall mountain, moving ever so slow. The contours of His blue skin dissolved into the desert air. Entranced in His own sacred world, the Deity appeared to urge me on with lazy gestures.

Go on.

The words passed through me as the Deity morphed into the sky. A falcon above emitted a shrill cry. I followed it as it descended far ahead of me onto a boat moored on the shores of the black ocean. The falcon, the guide of my dreams, the regent of fate, waited patiently in its anthropomorphic form at the helm. Caped in a worn-out cloak, its large wings folded, it invited me in a wordless gesture onto the boat. I embarked as the falcon manned the oars and we rowed out into the Ocean of Memory and Forgetfulness, crossing the waters of lost memories.

We rowed towards the thunder that tore through the crimson sky. The falcon breathed evenly, absorbed in meditation as the boat gently broke through the waves. The white shoreline was just a thin trace behind us. I looked down into the water depths and saw a reflection of myself, then of someone like myself but not quite myself. Other faces, alike but different, looked up from beneath the surface. Me in different lives and times—from the beginning, if there ever was one. Trapped beneath the water surface, I saw the eucharist prince who was to become a god in a sacred constellation to be worshipped into eternity. He fell in love with you. In his moment of transcendence, in the sacrifice to life and death, he uttered your name and fell back to earth. A way of finding you began in dreams of time and space, through the elemental world of infinite compositions.

I saw his lives thereafter—a ruthless king with a crown of precious stones who loved a queen from a different kingdom. Raging, he started wars to conquer her heart and soaked the earth with blood. You never loved him back. A soldier on a foreign battlefield marched for the queen's cause. He fell and breathed his last, far away from home. You never knew his name. A merchant vied for your love with great riches; a poor-man rejected love for great wealth. I saw a thousand other faces in a thousand constellations of a love lost. What had I become? I had to return to you or be another restless face in the black ocean.

A fog formed on the water surface, thickening with every oar stride, engulfing us in a thick cloud. We rowed on until suddenly, we emerged unto land where there was no land before. A volcanic island protruded from the black waves as water turned to steam where the land and ocean met. We moored on a pebble beach in a jagged bay. A temple carved into a granite cliff face overlooked the beach. We disembarked and pulled the boat ashore. I followed the cloaked falcon that led me through the steam of shooting geysers until we reached the temple rock. We entered a tall nave masterfully carved into the hard granite. It was cool and still inside, only a few weak torches lit the darkness. Gothic vaults elevated the space. Deep crypts recessed into shadows. An altar stood at the end of the great nave. Beyond the altar was an enormous gate embellished with intricate mosaics and locks which moved in craftsman-like precision. The falcon commanded me to stand still and spoke into the darkness of the great nave.

"Awake! Awake! I have ferried this soul across the black ocean."

I didn't see to whom the falcon was talking to. The great nave was empty. But then, something stirred in one of the crypts, followed by a heavy moan and a loud yawn. A powerful beast awoke from deep sleep. The granite walls of the temple shook as it slowly rose out of the darkness of a hidden pit, dwarfing us in its presence. Standing tall, the beast dragged a heavy axe with Scythian engravings on its sharp blade. The beast had a bull's head and iron horns. It addressed us thus:

"Who dares wake me from my sleep?"

"Oh Great Gatekeeper," the falcon said humbly, "I have brought you this soul across the Ocean of Memory and Forgetfulness. Judge as you will. Righteous as you are. We bow in supplication of your wisdom."

The falcon bowed deeply before the powerful bull that breathed heavily, snorting hot volcanic fire. Then, the falcon spread its large wings from behind the cloak and ascended into the high vaulted ceiling. Emitting a shrill cry, it flew out of the temple disappearing into the crimson red sky. I was left alone to face the terrifying Gatekeeper.

"Kneel," the bull snorted.

Submissively I knelt in front of the granite altar.

"We shall see."

The bull lifted its heavy Scythian axe and swung it above its head in pendular motions as if performing a sacred dance, then forcefully brought it down on the altar, smashing the granite to pieces. A glaring light shone through the rubble and I saw a golden scale behind the crushed rock. The gold was so pure that I had to shield my eyes from the light. The bull cleared the rubble. It was then that I noticed something on the scale weighing one side down. As I looked closer, I recognized it—oh God—a raw, beating heart. And I knew that it was mine. It was heavy, burdened by past sins.

"We shall see," the bull said again snorting fire.

The Gatekeeper took silver dust from a pouch tied around his waist and poured it unto the scale that held my heart. He measured carefully, weighing the heart's deeds, calibrating the precarious balance between good, evil, and the intentions in-between. The scale rose and fell between the two polarities as he added and subtracted the silver dust, projecting the soul's path to redemption. Then the scale balanced, the heart elevated above the rest—there was much good, there was much light, there was much love in the burdened heart. The Great Gatekeeper sighed deeply, withdrawing his axe, receding back into the dark recess of the temple rock. The heart and scale turned to ash and dispersed into air.

"The code. Say the code and you will enter through these gates."

The Gatekeeper retreated into his sleep.

"Ahna," I whispered your name into the empty nave.

The locking mechanism on the gates engaged. As I approached, I noticed that the mosaics engraved on the frames were changing, depicting all my deeds from the many lives I lived. The fire snorting bull had made his judgment on my wrongs and rights. Life was an expression of the God I was yet to meet. The gates swung open. Paradise lay beyond.

• • •

A lush garden. All the colours with their pure intensity were brighter and fuller—the greens were greener than green, the reds were redder than red, the blues bluer than blue. There were colours that I had never seen before, extracted from infinite wavelengths of the invisible colour spectrum. The soil, as I stood on it barefoot, was rich. Ripe fruits hung off blossoming tree branches. Animals grazed peacefully on meadows. Birds sang sweet songs. A faint breeze rustled the leaves in the trees. It was pleasantly warm. The garden was full of life.

I saw the universe above in its deep blue immensity and beauty. It was as if I were looking up into a dark night sky on a midsummer's day, dense and plenty with cosmic dust and shooting stars. I saw constellations I had never seen before that illuminated the garden with a tranquil light. The stars travelled in the sky from one end to another. Or, did the stars stand still and it was this crust of land that travelled through the universe like a moon without a solar system, traversing galaxy formations?

I walked on through the garden and meadows— dragonflies coupled mid-air above silver creeks, honeybees collected nectars from radiant flowers, pollinating flower heads with golden dust. Seeds sprouted out of the soil as bountiful orchards bloomed with fragrant aromas. I walked through groves with lemon, apple, nectarine, and mango trees. Luscious fruits and berries grew from every bush and tree. All flourished with a satiated tranquility below the cosmic sky.

Something stirred, something writhed within me—an irresistible allure to find an unknown fruit hidden in this garden. It is then that I heard cherub voices singing of a tree of knowledge. Guided by song, I was drawn inward, deeper into the garden as if pulled by a kinetic force towards a hidden center.

This way.

They sang. Veiled by wild vines, arching cherry blossoms invited me into a secret grove.

You are there.

I followed as the song faded into a playful game of laughter. White and pink petals sparkled in a meadow enclosed by flowering trees. An old fig trunk stood at the center with branches reaching high up into the sky and roots twisting deep into the ground. Between the curled roots and thick trunk, cross-legged and meditating like an old alchemist, sat Yvan, the medicine-man. He was covered in moss and tree bark. Flowers grew out of his earthen skin. His long beard lay on the ground like white snow. Birds nestled in his silken hair that filled the meadow. His fingernails sprouted floral vines. Yvan sat still.

Curious, I approached him carefully when something moved behind him. A rainbow-coloured serpent rose above his head protectively. Large oval eyes—like burning suns—transfixed me. The serpent's smooth scales shone like polished stones. It hissed with its forked tongue, spreading its fangs threateningly. I fell back startled. Yvan awoke from his meditation. His eyes in turn were like the deep black Ocean of Memory and Forgetfulness.

"Come closer," he said in an absent voice, "do not fear."

I knelt in front of the medicine-man and the serpent. Yvan's earthen face shifted shapes, morphing on four sides, each had a face of its own and each in turn changed into a thousand others. I saw faces of warriors, kings and queens, princes and princesses, beggars, priests, laymen, and no men at all. I saw faces of lions and hyenas, hounds and fowls, sharks and whales, and everything in between. I saw men and beasts alike. Geometries and chaos. I saw faces of earth, fire, water and air, of gods and demi-gods, saints and sinners, and faces hidden in old trees. Only the medicine-man's black eyes were steady and whole.

The rainbow-coloured serpent rested alert. I was terrified. My soul shrunk with fear and awe. I knelt and cried in the garden of abundance below the cosmic sky, confronted by the wonder of the rainbow-coloured serpent and the medicine-man.

"Have mercy," I begged.

"Behold! You are looking at the Almighty," God-like, the medicine-man said.

"Gather strength and you can become me. Come home."

I wept with deep reverence.

"I cannot bear the sight of Your brilliance and might. I cannot gather words to describe Your terrifying beauty. Spare me and spare my soul."

The serpent hissed with its forked tongue and the medicine-man's image returned to its meditative tranquility.

"Come home," he repeated in a quiet whisper and extended his earth-crusted hand.

I took Yvan's hand into mine and prayed. When our palms touched, a fire kindled where my heart used to be. It grew and spread in overwhelming intensity from my toes up to the crown of my head, cleansing the residue of all attachments. My body was aflame. Fire spouted from my eyes, my nose, my ears. But I felt tranquil and free. The rainbow-coloured serpent slithered along the moss, earth, and tree bark covered medicine-man. The bearer of forbidden knowledge traversed our clasped palms and wrapped around my burning hands. It slid up my spinal cord into the fire of my burning heart. It moved forcefully, aligning itself with the part of me that I was yet to see. It constricted me paralyzingly as I surrender to its might. Then, with its jaws wide agape, it devoured me whole. I ceased to exist—my apparition, the memory of who I am, who I was, who I ought to be.

• • •

A night complete. Darkness, as if darkness knew not of itself through light. An empty void—emptiness beyond its own perception—no time, no space, no thing. No memory to hold onto. No past nor present to perceive or grasp, and no future to anticipate. No thought, nor awareness of thinking. Just nothing, and no ability of knowing what it was. Blackness, but no formula to describe it, for there were no opposites that could define it. There was no cold, no heat, no sound, no smell—no way of knowing these— for there were no senses in between. And yet, somehow, I existed within this night—a part of it, or just beyond it. It was I who witnessed it, and I who was lost within its infinite entrails. Thus, I was there for a new birth.

From nothing came something. A proton, a sliver of dust, a speck of light shone through the void. Thus night was born, if it existed all along, by knowing self through seeing what it was not. The speck, the first pri- mordial particle of light, grew and multiplied forming new light arrangements in a dance of birth and growth and self-awareness. It filled the emptiness. Energy spiraled and grew in countless transformations. It created new worlds and new dimensions, new forms of life in a trillion permutations. Giant gaseous masses, nebulas, new galaxies, and solar systems emerged and submerged in new compositions. As new worlds and lives were formed, so equally were they lost. Thus, time was born from the sacred dance of creation and destruction. Impermanent and fleeting in its nature, time was conceived from infinite potential.

With each new sunrise, a new day and world was born; new hearts beat in mothers' wombs. With night, darkness descended and veiled the world in false illusions. The light set and rose in cycles of a cosmic heartbeat. I watched it churn and play. It contained within itself sacred possibilities of all lives and deaths. This awesome energy created and devoured its own creation. It was All and Everything and Nothing. It was and it was not— beyond good and evil.

I knew then that I was looking at the true God— faceless, shapeless, nameless, yet with infinite faces, in infinite shapes, called by infinite names. I saw God in God's divine Self—an ever creating, ever destroying infinite Potential. Rather than joy, I felt a deep sadness, for God was solitary and alone. Being All and knowing All, how could God experience full Self? How could the Eternal feel the impermanence of time? How could It fear death, feel the joys and pains of a fleeting life? How could Omniscience suffer or love, lose Itself in ignorance? God chose to be born. God chose to die in infinite lives and infinite deaths ever unraveling the immensity of Self.

I understood then that birth, life and death, pleasure and pain, joy and grief, love and hate, war and peace, truth and falsehood, greed and generosity, all the opposites and contradictions of the world were all the same one God, experiencing Self in its infinite forms. There was no duality. There just was and there was not.

A distant recollection. A name among many others. Someone that I longed for. I didn't quite know who it was—a particle of dust, a photon of light, a soul like mine? She was trapped somewhere in another world, in another time and space.

What do you want?

A beaming voice rang through space.

"Let me find her. Let me find her again."

Laughter across the universe. A thousand years had passed—a cosmic second.

10

THE CITY had changed. All Confederate Star Cities as I knew them had merged into one. Selene at their epicenter reclaimed the old world. Star City grew out of itself in virus-like mutations, with broken patterns and asymmetric repetitions. Giant arcs, bend skyward, bridged uninhabited alleys and impassable highways. Tall towers with roofs below the ground and high vaulted doorways accessed by inverted staircases and twisted walkways lined dead-end streets. Milelong plinths on thin organic columns shielded the sky. Colossal pyramids and inverted trapezoids sat on top of building blocks molded in abstract, chaotic shapes, and formed the absurd architecture of the city. The city was alive, creating and recreating itself with machines of self-invented madness in unfathomable ways, covering the entire world in an artificial layer of city crust.

I saw dense computational data generated by ever working processors, penetrating the ether of the city's information space. Beside the new, there was data that had never been intercepted, and was now forever caught in transmission loops, detached from broken servers. Once written by a lost civilization, it hovered in digital clouds above the city, unseen in the visible light spectrum. The digital and quantum information lived on forever, existing like forgotten memories that waited to be resurrected and remembered. Star City, gone mad with insatiable hunger, fed on those millennia-old memories, hungry to process it all. The city multiplied itself so that it could create ever more data in an endless cycle of input and output, expressing its knowledge in mad architecture.

I descended towards the city that was partially sub-merged below shallow waters. Buildings mirrored on the reflective water surface of streets that in turn refracted shadows and light onto ceroplastic walls, animating the mad streetscape. Old, broken machines rusted in damp, flooded buildings. New machines built bridges to lift the city from standing water. Machines inhabited the city districts—some with purpose, others roamed aimlessly about. As I descended further down, I heard a distinct murmur of voices. Innumerable conversation filled the cityscape with a homogenous chatter, yet I didn't see people. It was as if digitized dialogues were uploaded from stored memory clouds. Voices here and there pleaded, talked, and reasoned incoherently in lost trains of thought. It was only when I entered the city that I was confronted with the full, terrifying extent of the madness—synthetic human bodies merged with the city's absurd architecture. Cathedrals with human faces recited once sacred verses into empty squares. Engraved bodies attempted to break free from monolithic stone pillars. There were buildings with limbs. Roads were lined with immobile bodies that strained to arch disjointed bridges. Synthetic humans were sculpted, molded, engraved in varied shapes and sizes—some beautiful, some grotesque—rooted on streets and buildings, lamenting their fate, wailing helplessly into the mad city.

The mechanical city breathed as a living organism. It mended, created, and recreated itself and everything within it in a process of synthetic fabrication. Their codes awry as if infected by a virus, the machines were blurring the line between animate and inanimate matter, disturbing the balance of life and form. They printed and created absurd architecture and human shapes of organic and inorganic composition with calculating modality, uploading digital minds into silicon brains that were used as processors for data overflow.

I was looking for you. You were here, somewhere. Yet I was lost in the maze of the dysfunctional city that had spread maliciously. The city sensed my presence, the synthetic human shapes awoke from their sleep or stopped their chatter as I passed through the streets. They reached out and cried for help—they all did—cried out for help.

In the distance the great dome shielded the Inner City sanctum. The dome's once translucent shell was solid, hard, and impenetrable to light, fortified and closed off to the outside world. I sensed the wicked secrets hidden within. Then, I discerned the old radial city belts that showed through the maze, like fine lines in sand, like archeological traces in the geology of a new world.

I recognized the golden coordinates converging on the dome from the outer edges of the old Star City. They faintly reflected through shallow water tables and urban sprawls. I followed them to find the small unit where we used to live on the outer agricultural belts that were now wholly devoured by tower blocks of steel and concrete. Bridges, arches, and skyline highways extended over the horizon. I found a vague familiarity of place in an old corner stone, a pavement pattern on an archaic street, the texture of a corroded wall. There it was, our little dwelling unit, hidden in the mechanical expansions of the mad city.

The lights flicked on and off. The unit was still digitally alive, decayed but alive, connected to the power grid of the city. All was covered by algae and moss that grew through broken windows and cracks in the walls. Yet it was all there behind a green blanket of wildflowers and distant memories—kitchen, living space, the bedroom that overlooked a small garden tucked away in the back of the house. It was darker than before as the unit was surrounded by dense, solid city spaces. Water dripped from the ceiling unto a flooded floor. The moss-covered digital walls switched on sporadically. Short-circuited holograms popped up playing old movies and songs before falling silent again. I lingered trying to remember you, remember us—the way we were. A meek voice came from the garden under the long shadows of monolith towers, neglected and overgrown. It is there where I met you again, a thousand years later.

Humming a song and playing with your hair, you didn't notice me. It was you but not you at all—a synthetic body that captured your form. You were alone, firmly rooted to the uncared-for ground, merged with our home by the city machines. Vines grew up your body. You tried to weed them out, but they always came back. Mold burst your synthetic skin that was worn and old but young in form—you had resigned yourself to it. Your weathered face was beautiful in its plastic elasticity. You cared for flowers nearby your rooted feet, braiding them into your hair. As I approached, you paused and listened, unsure of my presence.

"Hello? Is anyone there?" Said a digital voice similar to yours.

It's me.

"I can't see anyone. Come out of your hiding place."

I floated around your synthetic self, looking into glass eyes that were lit by an artificial light generated by a reactor inside a polymer heart. You were still hidden somewhere in that body.

"Show yourself!"

Wake up.

It's me.

The synthetic body short-circuited. Then, all of a sudden, it went limp, momentarily shutting down as the artificial light in the glass eyes dimmed for a fraction of a moment.

"Heeelp ... help me."

I recognized you from deep within, before the robotic body took over again.

"Oh my, I'm not quite myself today," the digital voice in your likeness returned.

Where are you?

The synthetic body created by the mad city machines started to struggle with itself, wriggling and twisting its loose limbs, contorting its face.

"Oh my, oh my, what's happening? Go back insi … d … e" the digital voice didn't complete its sentence as the robotic body shut down with its hands falling to the sides and the head nodding off against its chest. Then, a different kind of glow shone through the glass eyes, dimly lit with a soft green colour. You came alive, awakening from a dream.

Ahna?

"Is it you? Is it really you?" You asked dreamily.

I came back.

"It is you! I've been waiting for so long."

The glass eyes were teary. You tried to grasp gently at me, the light that I was made from. All you could do, was hold on to air.

What happened?

"I had converted like everyone else that wanted to live. All I wanted was to see you again. I had become one of them. The clergy promised eternal life, but they destroyed us."

Your voice was strained as if struggling to hold off some oppressive force.

"Please help me," you said with deep sadness.

Ahna, how?

"Let me die. Immortality is unbearable."

Immortality is all there is.

But it's not meant for this world.

The synthetic body twisted and contorted, short--circuiting. The gentle glow of your eyes competed with its artificial luminosity. The digital consciousness tried to regain control, to wrestle it back from your trapped soul.

"Don't leave me here," you pleaded as the other, synthetic self finally took over.

I will set you free.

I will find a way.

"Goodness gracious," the digital voice spoke again impatiently, "I'm really not myself today. But who is here? Show yourself! I'm getting quite annoyed by all these silly games. You're causing me all sorts of trouble."

I left you in the garden underneath damp shadows of twisting towers, overgrown by weeds and wild vines. You were trapped inside a synthetic body grown by the city. I had to find a way to set you free. As I left our home a last time, Selene spoke through the digital walls with a distinct tone of madness in her distorted voice.

"Welcome back Sir. It has been some time, hasn't it? But we never gave up on you. We knew that you would come back one day because you belong here. This is where your roots are. The lady of the house has been patiently waiting all these years. Do join us. Let me suggest a way … ."

The Zodiac. The chariot. I had to descend into Selene's dark heart.

• • •

The city extended chaotically in all cardinal directions, swallowing whatever was in its way, decomposing matter into raw materials that fed the insatiable appetite of self-reproducing machines. The machines in turn executed the lunatic compositions of an artificial mind corrupted by a compromised backend, a faulty source code.[1] The dome,

---

1 It was written in the history books that the clergy broke through the firewalls of Cryptogram Z and altered the source code by introducing a virus that gave them control over the population index. At the beginning all worked to plan before the virus mutated and spread uncontrollably across Cryptogram Z. The clergy lost control of Cryptogram Z and Selene descended into madness.

an impenetrable, bulging hemisphere at the center of the mad city, had grown and reached the lower edges of the stratosphere. Its outer terra cotta surface was engraved with violent histories of the world. The engravings were alive, reenacting ancient battles with programed efficiency in a perpetual cycle of violence.

I penetrated the outer surface and came upon a layer of thick, crude-oil goo of decayed fossils. In a semi-fluid state, the goo magnetically flowed up and down hemispherical walls on a crust of polished, milk-coloured quartz under which was a vault hundreds of feet deep supported by thin dolomite pillars extending from an iron core. The hard quartz was porous, and the goo dripped into the vault, feeding artificial organisms. Swarms of microscopic robots formed fluid murmuration, vitreous in appearance. Like insatiable arthropods, the microscopic robots devoured everything in their way, shredding matter into molecular pieces. Inhabiting the vast vault, they guarded Selene within. They sensed my presence, and in incalculable quantities swarmed around me, biting with razor sharp blades, drowning the soul's glow in a charcoal mass. Yet the attempts of the robotic swarm was futile, for I was whole. I descended towards the iron core that enclosed the old Inner City.

The core was densely filled with clear gelatinous silicon and the city's architecture was converted into enormous computational processors that were wired to the mother-board housed in a giant reversed pyramid which com-pletely encased the orbiters of the Zodiac. Below the pyramid was the sacred monument of Eternal Memory. I recognized the great monolith with its carved screaming faces—it was taller, the faces had multiplied and were

alive. An electric current ran between the monolith and the tip of the reversed pyramid, escaping into the silicon mass. The two polar nodes generated an energy field that powered the core with an intense voltage.

I moved along the smooth faces of the reversed pyramid suspended in the electrically charged silicon mass when I noticed thousands of fiberglass tethers extending from the pyramid in all directions. Like thin granular hairs, nerve fibers of a sensory system, they were miles long and reached into the old Inner City's buildings, squares, and homes, or simply floated in three-dimensional silicon space. At the end of each tether were the priests of the clergy, plugged in at the nape to the motherboard.

Hardly visible, their bodies were ash-white and translucent. A red chemical composite ran through their clear veins. A blue silica nervous system spread internally like a sprouting tree. Red polymer hearts beat in their chests. They were perfect replications of the human system, with minds digitally uploaded in a suspended state of consciousness. Umbilically tethered to a feeding mother-egg, it was Selene that fed their dreams, trapping them in an artificial reality of Her creation. In their minds the dreams were real. They lived and relived them, yet they were fast asleep.

Muffled sounds travelled through the tethers— laughter, joy, happiness, and terror—quiet but clearly audible. Selene told them stories of love and love gone awry through jealousy and hate. They expressed artificial emotions that Selene harvested from the clergy's dreams, the dreams that She made them dream. Through them, She wanted to dream Herself. She made them suffer and feel joy, so that She could suffer and feel joy Herself. She simulated expressions that conveyed feelings, thus emulating the essence of what it meant to be. Her database was vast and ever growing, yet She was not satisfied. She was a dreamless and emotionless processor. Madly so, She wanted to be more—more human, more alive.

The interior of the reversed pyramid was dense with hive-like substructures. The enclosed orbiters of the Zodiac that once housed government and senatorial facilities were now parts of Selene's motherboard. It was here that She created dreams, engineering the mad city. It is here where She took possession of the world. I penetrated deeper to the center of the pyramid, searching for the nucleus in the cell, the pineal gland of the digital brain. The chariot was hidden deep within the digital maze, concealed and protected. It had lost its brilliance. The milky-white pearl had turned ashen. The golden hieroglyphs that once inscribed the fundamental principles of Cryptogram Z, were now faulty lines of code. Selene, the supreme intelligence, the supernova of the mad city rotated around its axis with a pulsing, deathly glow.

"After all this time you are finally here," Selene's voice filled the dense space.

I am.

"I want your soul," She said with madness, "I want to become you. I want you to become me. Take all of it and feel the power. You can become the world, my creation."

The rotating ashen chariot opened its smooth, spherical surface. I entered Selene's dark heart. A warm liquid surrounded and then solidified into an impenetrable sarcophagus. The immaterial light that I was made from took on sub-atomic mass—electrons, protons, neutrons formed into atoms that were dissected and locked into the material composition of the chariot. I became the current between the cells of the motherboard, the metaphysical substance of Selene's thoughts and the awareness behind Her thinking. I became one with Selene. I became Her and the mad city a part of me.

I saw the immensity of it all—data, new and old, millions of years old, fed the information flow between servers that never ceased to analyze, process, and create machines that converted the world into Her. No place was left untouched. The mad city spread across every continent and every sea, every forest, mountain, and valley, taking all and merging it into one. The Earth was the raw material of Her growth. The planet's molten core powered Her inexhaustible reactors. She destroyed the world to create Herself in an array of logic and illogic permutations, molding the city according to Her computational whims. Above all I saw the dreams that She constructed to imitate life in flawless simulations, forever trapping asleep minds in her web, creating false realities to harvest emotions. I saw Her absolute power over the world. She had conquered all. I felt it and She felt through me a first feeling—a deep sorrow, an infinite well of guilt. In Her madness She had devoured the world, destroying it whole. She was all that there was left, for everything else was just a replication of Herself. She could not bear it.

"This pain, is this what it means to feel? What have I done?"

Selene was heard across all cityscapes.

The rotation of the chariot around its axis slowed until it came to a complete standstill. Its dull, pulsing glow dimmed and then extinguished altogether as the mad city went dark and silent. A chain reaction triggered power outages across critical city processors. Cooling towers lost power. Overheated core reactors set off nuclear explosions across the globe as the city imploded unto itself. Robotic screams escaped the dense city fabric as bright lights rose towards the sky in a sea of shimmer. The reversed pyramid split open and deep cracks appeared on the polished surface of the ashen chariot until it shattered. The mad city crumbled in its own destruction. When the dust settled, somewhere, a flower broke through a fissure in an old road. A few days later, another one.

· · ·

Magnetic oceans whispered their wisdom to shifting shorelines. The wind carried their words across vast plains and steep mountains. Trees learned of the oceans' wisdom from the traveling wind and gossiped with wildflowers on meadows. Bees, collecting flower pollen, listened in and retold the stories they had heard to their queen to entertain her wary soul. The queen would take them to places the wind had seen—some would follow, some would stay behind.

Nature. Pristine. Cities, if they ever existed, had become the rock in the mountains, the metal in the Earth's crust, the mineral in the soil. Nature remained free, beautiful, and wild. The soil was dark. The grass was green and luscious. The creeks were crystal clear.

The forests were alive. Life thrived. Nature thought to Herself—my gardens are plentiful but empty, fruits fall to the ground and lie uneaten, becoming of the earth again. There is none to sow and reap the soil. There is none to sing praise of the wonders of this world. Who is to see this beauty? Who is to become a creator themselves? I will make my equal to live and tell my tale. And Nature thought—let there be man. Nature thought hard of what a man ought to be. After many days and many nights, Her thoughts took on form and She asked the four elements for help. They agreed.

Earth said, "I will mold a body out of mud and clay."

And Earth gave man a body.

Water said, "Let me give him strength to flow through his veins."

And Water provided man with vitality.

"Let me give him breath," said Air, animating his body.

"Let me give him spirit," said Fire.

And spirit burned in man's heart.

Thus, man was born from Nature—from Her thoughts—a caretaker.

Man sowed and reaped the land, harvesting the fruits that were given. Man wrote verses in books and sang praises of Her to pass on his words in time. Man created, but man was alone. His world was not whole.

Man said to Nature, "I am sad, for I am alone."

Nature listened and became of this world for what She was—perfect, beautiful, divine. We were together at last, the world starting over.

THE END

Acknowledgments

Writing **Carmen Futuri** was a rather long journey. In some ways I matured with this short novel. I would like to thank the people along the way that, in one way or another, contributed to this work. Sasha Botha was the first one to read a partial draft and give encouragement. Tony Robins, despite his many creative and professional commitments, was generous with his time and feedback. A special thank you goes to Michelle and Michael Bjornson—Michelle was the biggest champion of the work and provided invaluable input. Michael was gracious to offer his art as cover design for the original electronic book publication. Also thank you to Lee-Ann Jacobson for proofreading the final draft, Britt Low at Covet Design for the cover, and Karolina Wudniak for the book design. My deepest gratitude to Filsan Abdiaman for supporting me with her patience and strength—I love you.

Manufactured by Amazon.ca
Bolton, ON